To Mom, Dad, and Sis

CONTENTS

Dedication

Chapter 1: A Long Day, A Big Project	1
Chapter 2: Poor Old Man	8
Chapter 3: False Start	11
Chapter 4: History Lesson	16
Chapter 5: Here, Kitty, Kitty!	22
Chapter 6: 120 Whole Cents	29
Chapter 7: Sleaziest Kid Around	40
Chapter 8: Legal Trouble	42
Chapter 9: Scandalous	45
Chapter 10: Gone Missing	50
Chapter 11: Chaos	52
Chapter 12: A Man With a Plan	56
Chapter 13: Paper Refill	69
Chapter 14: Youthful Enthusiasm	74
Chapter 15: Age of Employment	77

Chapter 16: Ticket to Success	88
Chapter 17: Why the Long Face?	100
Chapter 18: A Particular Referendum	107
Chapter 19: Don't Worry About It!	112
Chapter 20: Victory	118
Chapter 21: Dream Come True	127
Chapter 22: Temptation	133
Chapter 23: Betrayal	136
Chapter 24: My Villain Origin Story	143
Chapter 25: Aftermath	147
Chapter 26: Too Much Trust	150
Chapter 27: Pick a Lock, Save a Friend	153
Chapter 28: Legal Trouble 2.0	157
Chapter 29: People Change	162
Chapter 30: Time Doesn't Heal All Wounds	164
Chapter 31: A Second Chance	166
Epilogue	174

CHAPTER 1: A LONG DAY, A BIG PROJECT
Dan

I stumbled down the stairs, my stuffed backpack keeping me off balance. It was a Monday, the start of yet another week of school. The weight of the world seemed to rest on my shoulders as I reached the last step and let out a tired sigh. School wasn't particularly challenging, but the monotony of it all drained my energy nonetheless.

"Dan! Hurry up!" my mom called from the kitchen.

"Coming, Mom!" I replied, my voice tinged with reluctance.

My mom was a dedicated doctor, working long hours from 8 am to 6 pm on days she was on duty. On the other hand, my dad was a realtor, his schedule more flexible but equally demanding. We lived in a small town west of the bougie Jeffrey Heights. Our neighborhood was relatively safe, but other parts of town carried an air of danger– I guess every town has its quirks. Despite its imperfections, it was a generally pleasant place to live.

SAMUEL PARIGELA

Glancing at the clock, I realized it was already 7:48 AM. I had to be at school by 8, and my typical walk took around 10 minutes. After devouring a rather uninspiring breakfast consisting of a single skinny banana, I trudged off to school, feeling the chilly air seep into my bones. The weather seemed determined to mock me on this dreary Monday morning, adding insult to the impending boredom that awaited me.

As I walked, time seemed to both drag on and rush by. It was hard to tell whether it was 7:56 or 7:58; my watch had fallen out of sync. Regardless, I found myself standing at the school gate, ready to step into the confines of another uneventful day. The gate emitted a soft creak as I passed through, entering the campus where a symphony of sameness awaited me.

Navigating the dull blue hallway, I couldn't help but notice how the building seemed to wither away. Layers upon layers of paint had been haphazardly applied to the floor, giving it a worn-out appearance. Some seniors even joked that the layers of paint were five inches deep, as if the accumulated history of the school manifested itself in the crumbling infrastructure.

By some miracle, I arrived at my World

History class a minute early. The door was already ajar, and I slipped inside. Ms. Wentworth, like most of my teachers, had a penchant for talking rather than teaching. I settled into my seat and gazed absentmindedly out of the window, only half-listening as she shared an anecdote about encountering a gigantic bug while walking her dog. Wow, it's almost like she walked her dog *outside*, in *nature*, where there are *bugs*.

While everyone around me feigned interest, I held steadfast in my belief that authenticity trumped conformity. It was better to be true to oneself than to pretend enthusiasm for something that failed to ignite any genuine curiosity within. With a resounding ding, the clock struck 8 AM, signaling the official commencement of the day's academic proceedings.

Ms. Wentworth, now fully focused on the lesson at hand, began by questioning our knowledge of the Mayans. The class collectively nodded, acknowledging our familiarity with the subject. However, when she probed deeper, asking about their place of residence, the classroom fell into a perplexed silence. One brave soul ventured a guess, confidently stating that the Mayans lived in South America.

Ms. Wentworth gently corrected him,

revealing that the Mayans were inhabitants of Southern Mexico, primarily located in and around the Yucatán Peninsula. Eager note-taking ensued as she retrieved a colorful map, its vibrant hues contrasting with the mundane surroundings. With a laser pointer in hand, she traced the contours of Southern Mexico, delving into the intricate details of this ancient civilization.

Despite my disinterest in the ramblings that frequently interrupted her lessons, the allure of a lost laser pointer caught my attention. In a not-very-rare turn of events, the pointer had slipped from her grasp, clanking on the floor before rolling under my desk. Curiosity got the better of me, and I examined the pointer more closely, realizing it was a multipurpose tool adorned with various attachments. I quietly added it to the collection of peculiar items I had acquired over time from Ms. Wentworth, who frequently dropped and promptly forgot about things. She would always mutter to herself that she would get it later, but never actually did.

The rest of the school day dragged on, each class blending into the next with a maddening monotony. Math class with Mr. Fitzpatrick offered no respite from the tedium. He was an enigma, a gruff and weathered old man whose teaching abilities remained shrouded in mystery. His scraggly facial hair only served to enhance his air of eccentricity, while his one-word commands echoed like primitive grunts.

Dressed in a flamboyant ensemble–a bright red shirt paired with a yellow tie–Mr. Fitzpatrick stood at the front of the classroom, ready to bestow his "wisdom" upon us. His version of enthusiasm amounted to the phrase "let's learn," the only time his voice betrayed a hint of excitement. As he droned on about probability, my eyelids grew heavy, threatening to plunge me into an impromptu nap.

After what felt like an eternity, the bell mercifully rang, signaling the end of yet another uneventful class. Science, PE, and Spanish followed suit, each blending into the next like an indistinguishable blur. It wasn't until my last class of the day, English, that a glimmer of hope emerged. The realization that school would be over in just an hour kindled a spark of anticipation within me.

With heavy footsteps, I entered the English classroom, the softness of the blue carpet beneath my feet muffling the sound. Taking my seat, I found myself lost in contemplation, staring absentmindedly at the intricate patterns adorning the floor. The red dots, meticulously spaced apart, formed an expansive blue ocean, teeming with hidden depths and untold stories.

Mr. Dengel, the English teacher, noticed my gaze fixed on the floor and interrupted my reverie. Startled, I snapped my head upwards, only to collide with the underside of my desk, eliciting an involuntary yelp of pain.

"What are you looking at down there, Dan?" Mr. Dengel inquired, sounding concerned.

Wincing as I rubbed my throbbing head, I hastily responded, "Uh... nothing, sorry!"

Mr. Dengel smiled, the corners of his eyes crinkling. "I like looking at patterns too."

Mr. Dengel turned his attention to the class, a mischievous glimmer in his eyes. "I have a project for you all!" he announced, met with a collective groan from my classmates.

However, Mr. Dengel's enthusiasm was undeterred by our lackluster response. He assured us that the project would be enjoyable, promising an exploration of our community's intricacies. The challenge was to research a topic of our choice, delving into something impactful that would resonate with the community. While he discouraged mundane subjects like food safety inspections or the number of fire hydrants per street (which honestly sounds kind of interesting), he encouraged us to venture out into the town, interview people, and truly engage with our surroundings.

As Mr. Dengel emphasized the importance of our research taking place outside the confines of textbooks, he pointed towards the city hall building visible from the classroom window. The town, though small, possessed a unique charm, exuding a relaxed atmosphere enhanced by the lush green mountains that framed the backdrop. However, beneath the idyllic facade, the city grappled with its fair share of crime and homelessness, highlighting the need for improvement.

With a deadline set for the last day of school, I pondered what topic would captivate me and allow me to contribute something significant to the community. Fire hydrants and food safety inspections were out of the question–I wanted to tackle something meaningful, something that would ignite change and resonate with everyone. Determined to embark on this mission, I resolved to take a walk the following day, seeking inspiration and unearthing untold stories that lay hidden within the folds of our city's tapestry.

CHAPTER 2: POOR OLD MAN
Mr. Fitzpatrick

The school day began like any other, a monotonous symphony of uninspiring routines and disinterested minds. I stumbled down the stairs, my weary body weighed down by the burdens of solitude. Loneliness had become my constant companion, a specter that haunted the empty spaces of my existence.

The weight of my shoulder bag pulled me off balance. There were no wife or kids to greet me, no warm embraces or joyful laughter to brighten my days. My solace, if it could be called that, lay in the realm of numbers and equations. Mathematics was my sanctuary, a refuge from the cruel reality that surrounded me.

As I made my way through the hallway, the vibrant colors of my attire stood out amidst the sea of drabness. The flamboyant hues were a feeble attempt to inject some vibrancy into my otherwise bleak world. The students' eyes followed me. They saw me as an eccentric, a peculiar figure.

But what did they know? They saw a teacher, a dispenser of knowledge and a symbol of authority. What could they know about the burden of isolation, of unfulfilled dreams, and bitter disappointments? The pittance I earned as a teacher barely kept me afloat, a constant reminder of the insignificance of my profession in a world that valued superficial success.

The students filtered into the classroom, their youthful energy bouncing off the walls. I observed them with a mixture of cynicism and resignation. They were a generation lost in a sea of distractions, their minds adrift in a digital abyss.

I knew that my role was merely to go through the motions, to impart knowledge to minds that were unwilling to receive it. Their disinterested gazes and half-hearted attempts at participation told a story of apathy and indifference. What joy was there in teaching a generation that valued instant gratification over intellectual growth?

Dressed in my bright, eye-catching attire–a red shirt that clashed with the yellow tie–I stood before them. My voice, tinged with sarcasm, echoed through the classroom. It was a defense mechanism, a shield against the indifference that surrounded me. My words were always laced with irony, every syllable leaving a metallic taste on my tongue.

Mathematics, my one true passion, was

reduced to a compulsory chore for them. They saw it as a means to an end, a hurdle to be overcome. They failed to grasp the beauty that lay within its complexities, the elegance of its solutions, and the universality of its language.

The bell rang. They were free, their minds unburdened by the weight of knowledge and the complexities of life. I, on the other hand, remained trapped within the confines of my own existence...

The students would forget me, their memories fading into obscurity as they moved on to the next chapter of their lives. I would be left behind, a forgotten figure in the annals of their education–maybe even a subject of hatred for those kids who really hated math.

Alone in the empty classroom, I cleared my throat, my voice echoing through the silent space. "Another day, another illusion of purpose," I murmured to myself. The weight of my thoughts settled heavily upon my shoulders, as I prepared to face the next class. I didn't get paid nearly enough for this.

CHAPTER 3: FALSE START

Dan

With a jolt, I crashed out of my warm and cozy bed, tumbling spectacularly onto the wooden floor. I stumbled into my closet, frantically yanking a sweater off its hanger. In my haste, I managed to pull a few hangers down with it, creating a chaotic symphony of clattering metal. Too rushed to care or even notice, I proceeded to bound down the stairs, taking them two at a time, like a nimble mountain goat on a mission–what missions would one have other than eating grass, though? Not the best simile, I will admit.

As I approached the front door, my mom, with her disheveled morning hair and a cup of coffee in her hand, looked at me with a mixture of surprise and concern. "It's really early–and it's Saturday," she remarked, her voice laced with curiosity. "Where are you going in such a hurry?"

Eagerly clutching my sweater, I barely contained my excitement as I replied, "I have this project for my English class. Our teacher wants us to explore our community and talk to people to find a captivating subject. So, I'm off on an adventure, I guess! Don't worry, I'll be back soon."

She offered me a gentle smile but couldn't hide a touch of worry in her voice. "Just be careful and don't get yourself into any trouble, okay?"

Promising to heed her words, I closed the door behind me, ready to conquer the world and unearth an extraordinary tale. Stepping outside, I paused to take in the scene around me. The morning air was crisp, and the sun cast a pale golden glow over the sleepy neighborhood. It was a moment of calm before the world awakened.

In my eager exploration, my eyes landed on a dilapidated old ice cream parlor nearby. Its faded exterior told stories of days gone by, yet there was a captivating allure to the place. The bright pink ice cream scoop on the sand-colored cone glistened, defiantly reflecting the feeble rays of the cold sun. I found myself drawn to its mysterious ambiance, wondering what tales lay hidden behind the cracked windows.

As I peered through the dusty glass, the scene inside remained elusive, shrouded in shadows and secrets. The weathered building itself, once vibrant and alive, now wore a cloak of grayish decay. But in my imagination, I could almost see its former glory–a deep blue facade, now concealed beneath layers of neglect. It reminded me of the worn carpet in my English class, carrying the weight of countless stories untold.

A sudden gust of wind, biting and sharp, snapped me out of my reverie, causing me to turn my head in search of respite. The sight that met my gaze was a monotonous stretch of houses and uninspiring buildings, an avenue devoid of the intrigue I sought. Doubt began to creep in, whispering that perhaps there was nothing remarkable to be found in this direction.

However, the tantalizing allure of the ice cream parlor persisted, beckoning me with its potential significance to our community. Ignoring the naysaying voice within, I tilted my head, shielding myself from the relentless wind, and embarked on a determined sprint to the next block. The building now stood right across the street, separated from me only by a surge of cars and trucks.

Checking for oncoming traffic with a mixture of caution and excitement, I seized the perfect moment and dashed across the road, feeling a surge of adrenaline coursing through my veins. Safely on the other side, I hopped onto the sidewalk, my steps resolute and purposeful. As I approached the storefront of the forlorn parlor, a sense of anticipation gripped me.

Peering into the window, I caught glimpses of a long-forgotten counter, its surface coated with a thick layer of dust, and a faded menu that clung defiantly to the cracked walls. Tables and chairs, once lively and welcoming, now stood in silent abandonment. Cobwebs draped the corners, as if nature itself was attempting to reclaim this place. The sight was a testament to the building's gradual descent into a state of decomposition, an echo of its former glory.

Despite the decay, my mind sparked with inspiration. It baffled me that such a striking relic hadn't been razed by the government. There was a story to be told here, a tale of neglect and resilience that could ignite the imagination of my English teacher, Mr. Dengel. With determination fueling my every thought, I envisioned the masterpiece of a paper I could craft, one that would undoubtedly sweep him off his feet.

Circling the weathered structure, my eyes scanned the walls, searching for any sign of access. To my delight, a vibrant bright orange door came into view, standing out defiantly against the somber backdrop. Its color was a beacon of opportunity, impossible to miss. Eagerly reaching for the doorknob, my hand closed around empty air–a cruel reminder of the building's deteriorating state. The doorknob had long abandoned its post, a casualty of neglect.

Undeterred by this setback, I pounded on the door with my bare fists, hoping it would yield to my insistence. But alas, my efforts proved futile. Just as despair began to settle in, a voice shattered the silence, freezing me in my tracks.

"Hey, kid! What on earth do you think you're doing? I'll call the police if you don't scram!"

Startled, I turned my head to face the source of the stern voice. It was a pedestrian, walking her dog and eyeing me suspiciously. Panic seized my heart at the mention of the police, the thought of being embroiled in legal trouble at the tender age of twelve quite frightening. I would never trespass!

Immediately, I retraced my steps, my dreams of uncovering captivating project material shattered like the broken glass of the ice cream parlor's windows. I trudged back home, all enthusiasm dampened.

CHAPTER 4: HISTORY LESSON
Dan

Resting my head on the windowsill, I gazed out at the world beyond, my heart heavy with disappointment and frustration. The day had been a whirlwind of emotions, beginning with hope and ending in despair. That ungrateful building had crushed my dreams in an instant, rejecting my attempts to breathe new life into its dilapidated walls. It had chosen rebellion over restoration, defying my vision of transforming it into a vibrant masterpiece, a beacon of inspiration for all to behold.

As I sighed in frustration, the sound of my dad's booming voice echoed through the house, calling me downstairs for dinner. Our cozy two-story home, outwardly grand but inwardly intimate, carried the voices of my loved ones to every corner. I cherished this closeness, the feeling that my family was just an arm's reach away, even when they were on another floor.

Joining my parents and grandpa at the table, I was greeted by my grandpa's affectionate smile– a smile that warmed my soul and made me feel cherished. As we settled into our meal, Grandpa's eyes sparkled with curiosity as he inquired about my day at school.

I slouched in my chair, still lost in the disappointment of my failed project. However, compelled by Grandpa's genuine interest, I tentatively shared the details of my English assignment–an impactful research project on our community.

His face lit up with excitement. "Something intriguing, huh? Something unprecedented?"

"Yes," I responded hopefully, because maybe he had a unique suggestion to salvage my project.

Grandpa furrowed his brows, his eyes fixed on the table as he delved into deep thought. He was a man of humor and wit, but when contemplation took hold, he became a pillar of silence. Minutes stretched on.

Finally, breaking the silence, Grandpa spoke with a mischievous glimmer in his eyes. "I think I have *juuust* the thing."

My fork clattered against my plate as I placed it down, eager to hear his revelation.

"Ya see," Grandpa began, "there's a place on the edge of town, at the intersection of Kern 'n'

Delano. It's a bit shady, but I believe it'd be the perfect fit for your project."

"What kind of place?" I asked, leaning in closer, hungering for every detail.

Grandpa chuckled, savoring the moment before exclaiming, "A bar!"

My mind raced to comprehend the concept. I knew bars were gathering spots for adults to drink, and the area around them was generally sleazy. My knowledge of them was limited, but Grandpa's mischievous grin urged me to explore further.

"A bar?" I questioned, my curiosity piqued.

"Yes, my boy, a bar!" Grandpa confirmed, his amusement contagious.

Confusion washed over my dad's face as he interjected, "A bar?"

Grandpa nodded, relishing the opportunity to share a forgotten tale. "Indeed, it is now a bar. But boy, forty or fifty years ago, it had a different identity–it was a library."

Surprise coursed through me at the mention of a word rarely heard in our small town.

Libraries were distant concepts, and the closest one lay many, many miles away, unheard of in our community.

Grandpa continued, his voice tinged with nostalgia, "That old library was a hub of life, where people of all ages gathered, forgin' connections, and immersin' themselves in the joys of learning. 'Twas more than a repository of knowledge–it was a vibrant community center."

Intrigued by the prospect, I leaned closer, my imagination running wild with visions of a lost era.

"Who owned the library?" I probed, eager to uncover every detail.

Grandpa's eyes glazed over as he delved into the past. "If memory serves me right, it was owned by a gentleman named Liam Caddel. Liam, a multimillionaire, homed up in a grand mansion and drove the most luxurious cars. The town was thrivin' under his influence, everyone knew each other through the library, and crime rates hit record lows..."

"But then," Grandpa's voice dropped, "Liam tragically passed away in a car accident, he just died, leaving behind uncertainty. Who would inherit the library? Liam had several children, and no one knew the fate of the beloved establishment."

Grandpa's narrative captivated me, the weight of the town's history pressing upon my shoulders. "The chair of the library's foundation announced that Liam's youngest son, Willis, would be the successor. Willis was an enigma to our community, his life shrouded in privacy during and after college. We presumed he would follow in his father's footsteps, but our assumptions proved painfully wrong."

Grandpa's voice brimmed with disappointment as he continued, "When Willis gained control of the library, he dismantled the foundation and disbanded the activities that brought us together. The vibrant essence of the place withered away, leavin' behind a mere shell filled with books. No more coffee mornin's, no more book readin's or inspirin' guest speakers. The library's patio, once a sanctuary overlookin' the beautiful landscape, became devoid of life."

I hung onto every word, the image of the lost library etched in my mind. His voice wavered.

"And then," he continued, sounding heavy with disdain, "Willis made his move. He decided to demolish the library, sellin' the books for profit, and built a bar in its place. Our community was powerless, too intimidated by his wealth and influence. He catered to the big spenders, promoted shady dealings, and focused on profit. Many embraced the temporary enjoyment of the bar, unaware of the lastin' contentment the library had offered."

Grandpa let out a long sigh, as if releasing decades of pent-up frustration. I helped him clear the table, our minds full of unanswered questions and unresolved emotions. Retreating to my room, I glanced out the window, the darkness settling over the world.

A determination surged within me–I had to visit that bar. But what would I seek? Whom should I approach to unravel the history hidden within those walls? Perhaps the manager or the owner held the key to the bar's forgotten past.

Tomorrow, I would find the intersection of Kern and Delano, visit the bar, talk to the manager, and write my paper. Easy A.

CHAPTER 5: HERE, KITTY, KITTY!

Dan

The next morning, I woke up with a renewed sense of excitement and determination. Ideas for my project swirled in my mind, and I felt a surge of confidence as I bounced down the stairs and headed to school. The sun beamed relentlessly, casting harsh rays on everything it touched and making it hard to read the road signs.

As I walked to school, my thoughts drifted to a memory from long ago. I used to wear a small, red baseball cap given to me by a student named Lukas Tinderdale. That cap had been my constant companion, accompanying me everywhere I went. However, one fateful day, while walking from my first period to math class, a strong gust of wind snatched my hat away. In a stroke of unfortunate luck, it struck the principal's face, leading to an unwanted trip to the principal's office. From that day on, I distanced myself from the red hat and avoided Lukas Tinderdale, for whatever reason blaming him for the incident, associating him with bad things.

After school, I returned home, feeling parched from the sun's relentless heat. I quickly grabbed a glass of water, quenching my thirst, and then remembered the curiosities I had stashed in my bag. I selected a useful item and stepped out the door, after letting my mom know where I'd be. My grandfather appeared from the living room, offering me his well wishes.

As I stepped outside, the sun's harsh glare greeted me once again, and I groaned inwardly. Determined to push forward, I repeated the names "Kern and Delano" to myself. Thankfully, I had a decent knowledge of our town's layout, so I turned right and continued walking.

The pristine sidewalks soon gave way to cracked and dirty paths, revealing a darker side of the town. The sun, while still present, seemed weaker, allowing me to look it in the eye and question its excessive heat earlier in the day.

After a while, I noticed a bright red light in the distance. I picked up my pace, squinting my eyes to get a clearer view. As I got closer, I could make out the sign that read "Caddel's Bar." Hope surged within me, and I ran eagerly toward the sign, arriving at a tan-colored building. However, I couldn't help but notice the suspicious-looking crowd gathered outside. They scrutinized me with wary eyes, which I found offensive. What had I done to invite their disdain?

The line to enter the bar was long and seemingly never-ending. Looking ahead, I estimated at least sixty people waiting patiently. I glanced at the sun, realizing that it was starting to get late. If I stayed in line, it would take forever to get inside. On the left side of the bar–almost behind it–I could see two men fighting. There was a smaller man with a goatee and a yellow shirt and a bigger man with sunglasses. They were grabbing each other's shirts and pulling and pushing. The smaller man grabbed a brick that was laying in the grass and threw it at the other man, who, diving, grabbed a brick himself and shoved it into the smaller man's face–that escalated quickly. The smaller man fell to the ground, and I winced. But the smaller man retaliated by grabbing the bigger man by the neck and pummeled his face. They continued throwing punches and bricks, and every time it seemed one of them was going to bite the dust, they got back up again. No one said anything for a while–it seemed this type of behavior was normal around here. Some of the people in line even cheered them on.

However, it was getting loud, and security had to come out and separate them. "Too much to drink, eh? Go home, you two!"

The men said some choice words to the guard and to each other, further escalating the situation.

The man in the yellow shirt turned and caught me staring with my mouth open. "Watcha lookin' at, kid?"

I quickly walked away and tried to find another way into the building. I wasn't about to get into any trouble today… What would my mother think if she heard I got in a bar fight?

I walked around far past the line to the back of the building on the other side, where I discovered four overflowing green dumpsters. Careful not to step on broken glass scattered on the ground, I scoured the area for a door. There were just bottles and broken bricks everywhere, but no door. My search proved fruitless.

Suddenly, I heard a loud "clang!" as my foot accidentally hit the back wall of the building. Startled, I ran backwards out of fright, trying to identify the source of the noise. Additionally, I was scared that the men and security guard would see me, as they were just a few feet away. I was only trying to find a more efficient way to get in, but they might think otherwise. Coming closer, my eyes fixated on what I had assumed was a solid wall.

"That's not a wall," I whispered to myself,

crouching down to investigate. As I touched it, I realized it was a mesh door, painted the color of the rest of the wall. Suddenly, a worn brick skittered past me, probably thrown by one of the men. Without hesitation, I pulled it open and slipped through below ground level, escaping the dangers outside and finding myself in a dim and humid room. I had successfully infiltrated the bar.

My plan was simple: find a way into the main room, locate the manager, or ask someone for the manager's whereabouts. I cautiously explored the room, taking shallow breaths to avoid the pungent smell that filled the air. I noticed stacks of sturdy wooden crates, most likely containing the coveted green bottles that attracted everyone to the bar.

My attention was drawn to a set of old and scratched-up brown cabinets in the corner, adorned with thick cobwebs. It seemed as though all the accumulated dust in the room had settled in those neglected spots. Curiosity got the better of me, and I decided to inspect the cabinets. Out of the five cabinets, the first two were empty, except for a few utensils. The third and fourth cabinets were completely devoid of any items, except for some spiderwebs. In the fourth cabinet, I even encountered a live spider, which met an unfortunate fate when I hastily closed the door on it.

With a sense of anticipation, I reached for the handle of the fifth cabinet. To my disappointment, it was locked with no visible mechanism. Determined to unravel its mystery, I searched for something to break it open. I managed to find a screwdriver but soon realized it was not powerful enough to open the sturdy cabinet. Frustrated, I spotted a box of nails and spare parts nearby, hoping to find a hammer. However, luck was not on my side, and I discovered everything but a hammer. Frankly, this was all offensive.

Suddenly, a voice broke the silence, startling me. "Who dat?"

I froze, listening intently as the sound of keys jingling filled the air. A small man emerged from a nearby door, his face covered in dust and shadows.

"Whatcha doing 'ere, boy?" he asked, his tone suspicious.

Nervously, I replied, "I... uh... could you let me in, sir?"

He chuckled. "You? Being 4-foot-1? How old is you? Nine?"

Straightening up, I felt a pang of hurt. "Why,

I'm twelve, sir," I responded, trying to assert myself. And I absolutely was *not* 4-foot-1, but 59 inches, straight up.

Amused, he reached for a light switch, intending to get a better look at me. "You're gonna hafta switch those numbers 'round to get in 'ere son,"

However, before he could complete the action, a red laser blinded him momentarily.

"Thank you, Ms. Wentworth," I whispered silently, grateful for the distraction.

"Here, Kitty, Kitty!" I screamed, and taking advantage of the temporary confusion, I moved past him. Using the pointer to guide my way through the dimly lit room, I climbed up onto the concrete behind the bar. The men were gone, but the pieces of bottles and bricks were still there. I ran up to the street past the ever-growing line. It was clear that I needed a better plan for my next visit, one that involved striding through the main entrance with confidence, like a true explorer on a mission.

CHAPTER 6: 120 WHOLE CENTS
Dan

I went to my room the next day after school and sat down on my bed.

So... in order to enter the bar, I needed to be older. I needed to be 21. The thing is, by the time I became 21, it would have been way past the due date. While Mr. Dengel was generally flexible when it came to late work, I was pretty sure turning the project in nine years late might be stretching it a bit too far.

I pulled open the wooden doors of my closet. I shuffled through my clothes listlessly, finding nothing that could possibly help me in this particular endeavor. Nothing here could help me look older than my age. How would I look old? I, for one, definitely don't look the part of a 21-year old person. Even if I were to wear my dad's clothes, I would just look like a seventh-grader with really big clothes. And if I were to wear grandpa's clothes... wait. People get smaller once they're really old, right? So, if I were to dress like an old person, I could maybe sneak in without anyone noticing. One thing, though; I would need gray hair. A wig. Something nice and big to cover my face–along

SAMUEL PARIGELA

with sunglasses, of course.

The next day at school, I hesitantly decided to consult the sleaziest kid around to help, the giver of the red hat–Lukas Tinderdale. He had a way around everything. I looked for him during lunch in the cafeteria, near the benches, and on the grass behind the school. He was nowhere to be seen. Suddenly, someone slapped my back.

"Woah!" I exclaimed, turning around to see Luke.

"What's up, Dan?" he said, and started to run off. He was trying to play tag or something, but I showed my uninterestedness by standing where I was, stone-faced.

"Luke," I said, walking towards him. He stopped and turned around.

"What?" he asked, playing uninterested back.

"Do you have any, uh, old people disguises? Like a wig and all?" I asked in a hushed tone.

"Well... why?" he responded, clearly not expecting that from me.

I stared into his soul.

"Okay, man, I ain't judgin', but… whatever," He said, taking a step back. "Yeah, I do. Like, I don't got a set from Kroger or something, but I think I have a couple, um, items that I can mash together and give you."

"That'll do!" I said.

"Hold up there, now. How much are you gonna give me?"

"I mean, it's not like I'm keeping it. Just for a day,"

"Labor charges? Shipping and handling? Custom bundling? I don't think a 'zero' would work too well for that," he said. Groaning, I reached into my ever-filled pocket and fished around for a bill or two.

"I got a buck," I said. "Oh, and twenty cents."

"A buck and twenty… so that's forty cents for labor, forty cents for shipping and handling, and another forty cents for the custom bundling? Well, brotha, I don't think forty cents for the custom bundling is gonna do it. It ain't gonna close the gap if you know what I mean. All this 'custom' stuff– it doesn't come too cheap with inflation and all,

SAMUEL PARIGELA

exceeding one's monetary limits to custom-make things. These manufacturing costs, soaring like your heretic apathy right now, while wages stay the same, you know? Forty cents a job? I woulda charged the same a while back, when there weren't no inflation. You wouldn't understand anyways, 'cause–"

"Look, let me put it this way: 120 whole cents!" I cut in after hearing him talk about nothing for so long. He had such a strange personality.

"It's the same, though," he responded, cross.

"It's all I have right now, though," I countered. "And that's all you'll be taking," I added.

He rolled his eyes. "Give it to me now, then. They better not be fakes or some of the old stuff, I'm no collector. And I'll meet you tomorrow as soon as lunch starts, right here."

I gave him the money and went off to my next class, as he examined the coins from every conceivable angle.

The next day, I ran from class to the same spot, under a tree next to the school office. I saw Luke with a tote bag, wearing a small red hat. I tried not to look at it.

"I got your stuff," he said. "A bunch of stupendously convincing threads and rags and a whole mixture of goodies and extras–a manager's special," he eccentrically declared. I peered into the bag. All I could see was a mess of gray on top and some other clothes that were covered by the grayness. Luke could be an excellent salesman. I took the bag and kept it with me for the rest of the day.

As I walked home, the sun beamed as hard as it could on me, being particularly brutal. I stopped and put the bag down. I reached inside of it and searched for any 'goodies' that could be of any avail right now.

I saw a flash of red and reached for it, only to unearth another red hat. "How many red hats does the kid have?" I whispered.

As soon as I went home, I fully examined the contents of the tote bag by spilling it all on the floor in front of my bed. The "threads and rags" were... colorful, to say the least. I saw a yellow coat, a bright green sweater, a vibrant blue tie, a wig, and a stick-on mustache that matched the wig. I didn't see any 'goodies' or 'extras'. Maybe he was talking about that hat.

I also added my own item to the collection–some wireframed sunglasses I found a while back behind the school. They would complement the set perfectly, and further conceal my face as well. I put on the sweater and the coat over my own t-shirt and a pair of shorts, then thrust the wig on top. I stuck the mustache above my mouth and adjusted it so that it was even. Looking in the mirror, I realized that I appeared suspiciously like Mr. Fitzpatrick, my math teacher. I grabbed the screwdriver from my last visit to the basement not wanting to keep it, as that would be stealing. I pressed the sunglasses into my face, and got ready to go.

"Hello. Why, hello there, fella. Hm, what's your business here? Hello. Hello." I practiced my gruff voice, trying to make it sound as mature as possible. "Now, don't you mess with me like that, whippersnapper. Get in the workforce and grind, ignorant youth! Hustle!" I chuckled. *I'm pretty good at this.*

I walked the distance to the bar, making sure the stick-on mustache didn't fall off. The line wasn't too long. I stood behind a gentleman in an untucked dress shirt and loose jeans. He was humming a jolly tune and swinging from side to side, on the beat.

I looked forward and saw someone at the door wearing a shirt with the bar logo on it. I looked closer and saw that the woman was checking small, rectangular cards that the people in line gave him. They must be IDs, and that's how they know the entrants are 21 years old or older! I didn't have an ID, but I surely looked old enough to be more than 21. If they wanted my ID, it'd gotta be a joke.

When I reached the door, the bar staff member asked for my ID, and it went like this;

"ID please!" She smiled pleasantly.

"Why, hello there, fella. Now, don't you mess with me like that, whippersnapper!" I internally face-palmed.

"Sir, I need to see your ID,"

"Why? I'm a little old man! Born in 1929, a child of the Great Depression and Prohibition!" We had learned about that the day before. Ms. Wentworth would be proud.

"Sir–it's policy, we can't let you in without an ID." Uh-oh, she was no longer smiling, much less smiling pleasantly.

"I... Forgot it! At home! Oh, my age-related memory loss!" We learned about that in science recently during the life stages unit. I was proud to make real life applications of it.

She made a face, looking rather concerned. "I'm sorry, sir, but it sounds like the bar isn't the place for you. Do you remember how to get home?"

I stared at the brick wall, offended. "Of course I do! Now let me in!" This was out of character for me, but I didn't pay 120 whole cents to Lukas Tinderdale for nothing.

"HURRY UP OLD MAN," People in line were getting frustrated.

"Sir, I *will* call security." She looked very upset.

I was frightened. *Security*? What would my mother say?

"Understood. Have a good one young'un. Get in the workforce and grind, ignorant youth!" I smacked my hand over my mouth. I really just said whatever, didn't I?

I hobbled, as old people do, around to the back of the bar, determined to get in no matter what. I'd just have to use the same method as last time.

Now, I noticed a sign that said 'NO TRESPASSING' with a little triangle caution sign over the mesh door that I entered through. Was that there before? They were trying hard to keep me out. I rummaged through the dumpsters and grabbed one of the glass bottles. Gotta be the character, the very drunk character.

As I slid down the boxes, I noticed that it was darker than when I was last in here. I turned on the flashlight that was on Ms. Wentworth's laser pointer and in an instant it was much, much brighter than when I was last here. Once I reoriented myself, I found that I was again attracted to the cabinets. I went back to the mysterious fifth cabinet and tried opening it again, to see if I got lucky this time.

I didn't, but I saw the screws holding the cabinet up. I hadn't seen those before! How did I miss them? I realized it was thanks to the angle I was holding the light at– before, the screws were engulfed in the shadow of the cabinet itself, created by the sun–which itself was barely there, mostly blocked out by the trees and the mesh. I put the bottle and the light down on one of the boxes and started unscrewing the cabinets with my trusty screwdriver.

The screws on the fifth cabinet were the tightest. Without hesitating, I fully unscrewed it and took it off the wall. A small piece of paper fell out. A treasure map? That would be cool. I folded the paper and madly screwed the cabinet back on to the point that the drill points started to wear out. I heard something, a door opening.

"Well, by golly, who dat down there? If it's that 9-year-old rat again..."

It was the same guy–I literally told him I was twelve! I shoved the paper far under every layer of clothing I had on and attempted to climb back up the boxes and out, but he stepped in and blocked my way out. I didn't have time to get the laser out, and even if I did, it probably wouldn't work on him the second time. I had to go into old, drunk person mode now.

"Whatcha doing here, old man?" His eyes widened. "Fitzpatrick? I didn't know you was a drinker!"

Come on. Now I had to maintain an identity. "Why, sonny boy, I was been a-drinkin' and," I paused for a deep, heavy laugh, swung the bottle around, and continued. "I know you must know how much the bottle can do to a man, ha ha! I was boozing up by the dumpsters and, lo and behold, I finds me here, sirrah! How'd I get here? How does I get my sorry self out? Why, I knew not these things when I first arrived, but now I return to my normal self, and am able to speak to you in such a manner," I said. "Ah, I love math, the probability of me loving math is 100%..." I was extremely pleased with my performance, but I contained myself.

"Well, old fellow, I'm afraid I must call the cops, 'cause it says here, 'NO TRESPASSING'.

Well. That took a turn. My mind raced as he proceeded to call the authorities. There wasn't much I could do as the on-site cops came and stuffed me in their car. We sped off, going the opposite direction of my house. The first thought that came to mind–what was I going to tell my parents? That their only child got his first imprisonment at the tender age of twelve? Oh my. I'm in legal trouble.

CHAPTER 7: SLEAZIEST KID AROUND
Lukas

As I examined the coins Dan had given me, my mind wandered to the peculiar nature of my interactions with him. Dan was a peculiar character himself, always so serious and focused.

I couldn't help but wonder about his motivations. What does a person like him need a disguise for? This question swirled in my mind as I examined the worn-out coins in my hand.

Outside of our unusual arrangement, I had my own set of interests and hobbies that occupied my time. While some considered me the "sleaziest kid around," there was more to me than met the eye. You see, I had a knack for tinkering with things, taking them apart, and finding creative solutions to everyday problems.

In my free time, I would often retreat to my makeshift workshop in the basement of my house. There, amidst a chaotic jumble of tools, spare parts, and half-finished projects, I would lose myself in my passion for invention. It was my sanctuary, where the constraints of the world faded away, and I could let my imagination run wild.

Huh. This dime was a 1911 Barber! I pulled out my magnifying glass to observe the ridges–Dan better not have given me a phony. I wonder how much it'd be worth at the pawn shop–probably a few dollars at least.

Building contraptions, modifying gadgets, and experimenting with various materials brought me a sense of fulfillment and purpose. It was through these projects that I felt a glimmer of control in a world that often seemed unpredictable and chaotic. There was a satisfaction in taking something broken or outdated and breathing new life into it.

I couldn't deny that there was a part of me that enjoyed playing my role as the sleazy, street-smart kid who always had a solution. It gave me a sense of power, knowing that I possessed knowledge and skills that others sought.

As I tucked the coins securely into my pocket, a mischievous grin played at the corners of my lips. Meeting Dan today was interesting, to say the least. I wondered what he would make of the disguises I had gathered, and if he noticed that I'd been inspired by Mr. Fitzpatrick–a fashion icon.

CHAPTER 8: LEGAL TROUBLE

Dan

The policemen escorted me through the imposing gates of the local jail, its tall gray walls stretching high into the sky. The building's numerous windows, though small, added to its intimidating presence. As we approached, a shiver ran down my spine, and I couldn't help but feel that once you entered this place, you might never see the sun again.

The police car came to a halt in front of the massive structure. I mustered up the courage to push open the heavy car door, my heart pounding in my chest. Stepping out onto the tan, brick path, I found myself flanked by the police officers, who guided me toward the entrance. The exterior had given me a foreboding impression, but as we crossed the threshold, I was surprised to find that the interior wasn't as grim as I had expected.

Inside, the atmosphere was surprisingly clean and orderly. It defied the scummy and dark depiction often found in books and novels. We entered a room where a rough-looking man sat behind a desk. I presumed it was the registration area. He eyed me with suspicion as they took my mugshot, capturing the image of my disguised appearance, booking me in. Afterwards, I was handed a set of bright orange clothes and directed toward one of the changing rooms. Despite the change, I decided to keep the wig, mustache, and sunglasses on, maintaining my old man persona. And I was sure to keep the piece of paper underneath my wig.

Finally, the guards led me through a maze-like series of corridors, my heart sinking with each step, until we arrived at my new "home" for the next day: holding cell number 3. I entered the small, dimly lit space, its cold concrete walls and unwelcoming aura emphasizing the severity of my situation. Collapsing onto what the guard called a "bed", I expected some degree of comfort, but I was immediately repelled by the mattress, or rather, foam rectangle's coarse and scratchy feel.

I ran my fingers along the rough surface, contemplating the events that had led me to this unexpected predicament. How had a simple adventure to complete a school project landed me in a jail cell? The gravity of my actions and the harsh consequences now dawned on me. Trespassing, something I had previously considered a light offense, had unexpectedly transformed into a serious transgression rather than just a fine. The laws in this jurisdiction were certainly intriguing, to say the least.

Removing my damp prison boots, I resigned myself to the reality of spending the night in this unfamiliar and unforgiving environment. As I settled onto the uncomfortable bed, the threads scratching against my skin, I knew that my own house would remain a distant dream for the night. The darkness enveloped me, and I braced myself for a long and arduous night in holding cell number 3, uncertain of what the future held in store.

CHAPTER 9: SCANDALOUS
Dan

I woke up to a pleasant light shining in my face. I scratched my head and remembered that I still had the wig on.

"That's a mighty fine wig," I thought to myself.

I touched the area under my nose and felt the soft, faux hairs of the mustache. It had stayed on as well, apparently.

Sitting up now, I looked outside the window. A sunny, beautiful day outside greets me. The air was fresh and there was but one small cloud in the sky–it, too, fleeing the wide expanse of bright blue.

I lay back down in my bed, but the coarse texture of the bed made me get back up. I wondered what my parents were thinking. They must have been petrified. And my poor grandpa. I can't even imagine how he must have been feeling. If there's one thing I had learned, it was how to go to prison at twelve years old.

The matter at hand, at that point, was how to escape. There were a couple options–some viable, some... not so much. Firstly, I could try to snake my way through the window. If I were to take off the disguise Luke so graciously gave to me, I could wiggle my way to freedom, hoping there isn't a guard down there. Or a dumpster. Or snakes. A drawback to the plan (besides those mentioned just now) is that I might not fit. There were thick bars blocking anyone from trying to get out.

However, this prison was intended for adults, and I was a relatively thin kid. But, I still might not fit. Even if I thought I could manage to go through the bars, it would take effort to slide through, and if a guard sees me trying to get out, I would be done for. I'd probably be put in solitary confinement, or some torture room. And that's not good. The worst case scenario was me getting stuck in the bars while trying to escape. I could already imagine a 12-year-old boy halfway in, halfway out, writhing in pain being stuck, but unable to get out. The thought itself is frightening. I couldn't remember what they said my bail was, but I wasn't about to make my parents pay it.

I finally conceived one last plan. It would be a tough one, but at the look of things, it was the most feasible.

A guard opened the cell about an hour later. He was short and stubby, with a bald, egg-shaped head and messy stubble on his face.

"Hey," he said in a gruff voice. "Lunch."

"Uh, so I want to tell you something, sir," I said in my regular voice. He raised his eyebrows.

"W-What?"

"So, this whole thing here is a disguise. I'm not actually old, I'm just a kid. You see, I'm… twelve." This was my plan, to simply fess up.

He looked stunned. Shocked. Like the world turned upside down. But he then proceeded to laugh the most light-hearted, unserious chuckle I could have expected from him.

"Okay… kid. Tell you what: I'll let ya go."

It's that easy?

"Wait, what?" I responded, overwhelmed.

"I mean, you shoulda told us before, but, like, I guess you really shouldn't be here, without a doubt. So, I can let you go."

"Thank you so much, sir!" I exclaimed.

"No problem, young man," he said, beckoning me out the door.

They could just free me if they want? Nothing legal involved? Nice.

The men at the table gave me my stuff and I changed back into my old man clothes. I took off the jacket and the wig so I didn't look so much like an old man.

"Off you go, now, kid," the guard said.

I ran as far from the prison as I could in one breath, knelt on the sidewalk, took out the paper and laid it flat on the ground. It read, "Last Will and Testament of Liam Caddel".

"Wait," I whispered. "That's the bar owner's father! The millionaire who owned the library!"

I scanned the document for "library" and found it nowhere except for one of the last lines. It said, "I direct the library which I own to be given to my son, Willis, that he may keep it a library all his days and instruct whomever he gives the library to to keep it a library as well. If Willis does not keep it a library, I request local authorities to assume control over the library."

Hold up. But Willis turned the library into a bar! He didn't listen to his father's last will and testament! He hid it! What do I do? Who do I tell? I had found myself a scandal!

CHAPTER 10: GONE MISSING
Mom

The day had been long and exhausting–nothing unusual for a doctor. As I turned the key in the lock and stepped inside the house, silence struck me with an unnerving force. The house felt empty, void of the happy greetings of my son.

"Dan? Danny, are you home?" I called out, my voice echoing through the empty rooms. No response came, and a flicker of concern danced in the depths of my heart. I rushed from room to room, searching desperately for any sign of my son, but he was nowhere to be found.

Panic tightened its grip around my chest as I called for my husband, my voice trembling with worry. "Have you seen Dan?" I asked, desperation lacing my words. He came out of the kitchen, his eyes mirrored my growing apprehension as he shook his head in confusion.

The neighbors were consulted, and their puzzled expressions mirrored our own. None of them had seen Dan, and a cloud of unease settled over our usually close-knit community. I dialed various numbers repeatedly, my trembling fingers struggling to hold the phone steady, but all my calls went unanswered. Fear gnawed at the edges of my mind, imagining all the possible dangers that could have befallen him.

Hours turned into an agonizing wait as night enveloped the world outside. With each passing minute, my heart sank further into my chest, aching with worry for my precious son. The unknown kept me from sleeping, the clock ticking almost menacingly.

Finally, as the first rays of dawn began to break through the darkness, I heard the sound of the front door opening. I had been on the phone with my mother, crying to her about what could have gone wrong. I turned with a mixture of relief and trepidation, my heart racing in my chest, and promptly dropped the phone.

There stood Dan, disheveled and weary, but safe.

CHAPTER 11: CHAOS

Dan

I wildly ran home, arms flailing like a maniac. I needed to tell my parents! I stopped at multiple locations, out of breath. Exhausted, I crashed in front of the door on the front porch. I waited a minute to catch my breath and then knocked.

My mom opened the door, with a phone glued to her ear and tears in her eyes. Oh. I had forgotten that my parents didn't know where I was. I was so caught up with being in prison and going to the basement that I forgot about my parents who were probably freaking out.

My mom's eyes got bigger than I had ever seen them and she dropped the phone in her hands to the floor. It didn't break, thankfully.

"Dan?!" she cried as a guilty feeling shot up my throat.

I was not sure what to do. Everything seemed happy and delightful outside. The sun was out. There were butterflies of various colors going about without a care in the world. But inside... It was a whole other story. There was the phone on the ground, my mom looking distressed, my dad on another phone saying something rapidly, and a whole lot of general chaos.

I saw my grandpa come out of another room. His eyes went wide and his worried expression turned into a huge grin. He knew that panickedly throwing questions at me would just make *me* panicked as well, so he remained calm, at least on the outside.

"What's with the mustache?" He asked as my parents whipped their heads around to see.

"It's... a long story," I responded, peeling it off of my face.

"Tell us over dinner," he said, and I went to help set the table. It was an odd feeling, doing something so normal after having the most frightening experience of my life. I looked at our silver cutlery and can only think of the basement, where I got caught twice, arrested once, and slipped out easily the last time.

After the table was ready and we began to eat, I took a deep breath and began retelling my adventures. From the cabinets to the jail cell, and my incredible revelation.

I took out the paper and showed my astounded parents.

"It is the last will and testament of Willis' father, Liam Caddel."

At this point, Grandpa, who was already staring at me in disbelief, was now gawking at me incredulously.

"Hold on there, you found his will? What? Could you pass that over for a second?"

I gave Grandpa the will and he got his reading glasses. "Okay... Caddel beach home left to Jeremiah... yeah, yeah... money in his bank account to be divided equally among the children..."

"Wait," I interjected. "Read the last sentence. Or maybe the one before it. The one about the library, Grandpa!"

"Library?" He looked down and peered closely, squinting his eyes. His eyes went big. He looked at me and showed me the last paragraph.

"It–It says to keep the library a... library?" he said, astonished.

"Yes, that's what it says!" I eagerly responded. "He clearly says that the library needs to stay a library."

"But that crook Will! He learned nothin' from his father. Nothin'. Actually, I take that back. You know, learned one thing, and he learned quite well," he says and chuckles. "The know-it-all learned how to farm dollars. And he has a talent for it. Where he goes, money follows. In most respects, I would say that's a good thing for him; it's a knack that can go a long, long way. But he let it get in the way of something valuable to this town. This place we all love. Makin' money ain't a bad thing, but Will chose the profitable route over the route better for us in the long-term. I mean, *of course* a bar would be more profitable than a library. There's no doubt over that.

However, bars can only harm a community. They profit off of folks' addiction to alcohol, and that's just not right. And when you consider the alternative–keeping the library–the only sensible decision is to not build the bar. It keeps the town safer, too. We'd have less drunk folks off the street. And less crime. The library kept us all together. Like I mentioned before, everyone knew everyone. But now... I really don't know, Dan. I really don't know."

CHAPTER 12: A MAN WITH A PLAN

Dan

There was a moment of silence.

"What can we do?" I asked in a hushed tone.

"I just said that I don't know. In this world, money is power. We have less money than the little chap, so we're powerless."

"But we have evidence that he's going against his father's will," I answered, holding up the will and pointing to it.

"And then what? Will he lift his hands and fess up? I don't think it's going to be *that* easy..."

"No; but read what else it says in the will. Mr. Liam Caddel specifically said that if his son didn't keep it a bar that it should be taken away from him!"

"Yeah. What if he says, 'so what'?"

"Uh... that's a good question." I stopped to think. "Wait, we could tell the mayor and city officials. They could surely do something!"

"Sorry, I'm being the Devil's Advocate here, but would they *really*? Would they care, even? In the grand scale of things, the bar is being more profitable than a library would. Why, the library was a non-profit. It made no money. Nothin'. All the money they ever got went to The Foundation, which took care of facility costs–which includes things like water and electricity, getting books, and organizing meetings. Any extra they got in a year went to charity and they would start from zero again."

I shrugged. "If it's our only option, it doesn't hurt to try."

"You're right."

"Honestly, I'm lucky they still gave me my screwdriver when I came out of prison," I said, laughing quietly.

My mom interrupted. "Wait, so you *actually* went to jail?" she asked, eyes full of surprise.

"Uh. Yeah." I responded uneasily.

"Seriously? You actually got incarcerated?"

"I did."

"But why?"

"The basement said no trespassing, but I just... went in."

"Wait, so it was actually *your* fault?" she questioned, raising her eyebrows.

"Well, it was my *curiosity*. I wanted to see what was inside of the cabinet. And look what I found!" I pointed to the will and grinned. "And wasn't it worth it? I found so much new information! Why, I found a scandal!"

"But, what are we going to do with it? Isn't that technically stealing?"

"We can show it to... people! And I, well–it's for the good of the community..."

"Ok, fine. But who do we show it to, exactly?"

"Folks in our neighborhood! We can tell the man at the grocery store, the people next door. We can tell everyone we know! Let's start an uprising!"

Thankfully, my parents didn't say anything about my fresh criminal history, and we finished eating.

The next day, I went off to school with a feeling of excitement inside of me. I discovered sensational news!

I walked to my English class and sat down. As the bell rang, signaling that class had started, Mr. Dengel asked us how far we had gotten with our projects. One kid raised her hand and said that she was writing about a pizza place on the other end of town that had been here since 1901. Another kid claimed to have found a gold mine under city hall. I kept my mouth shut and sat quietly, smiling at my own good fortune as other kids talked about theirs. They all thought that they had saved the world. Each one of them thought they had an immeasurable amount of luck. Frankly, I saved our town. And to be honest, I did have quite a bit of luck–aside from getting caught and going to jail, at least. I had a much better story than they did, and I was bound to get better feedback. The paragraphs to write would be easy. I could just ask Grandpa a couple more questions, and everything would be in good shape.

At home, I saw my grandpa showing my dad something from a book. I stopped on the second-to-last stair and took a look at the book. It was a deep orange color with words engraved in gold on the side.

"So the prison is over here and the, uh, bar..." Grandpa paused and skimmed his finger through the page on the book–presumably some sort of map–and stopped at a specific spot. He looked at Dad and said, "There." Dad squinted his eyes and focused on the point on which Grandpa was pointing to. I walked over to where they were sitting and sat next to them. They took little notice of me, if any, and continued their conversation.

"So the bar is right on Kern, huh?" Dad asked.

"Yeah," Grandpa responded. "Kern, and, eh, Delano."

So they were talking about me and my trip to the prison. I felt uneasy, as I had never liked it when people talked about me in front of me. They still continued to ignore me. A little irritated by it, I started speaking.

He turned to my dad and they continued talking. When they finally took a pause, I started.

"Who can I tell about the will?"

"I'm sure you can think of plenty of creative ways," he said, and turned back to his conversation.

Frustrated, I went back to my room. But I sensed that my dad was just deeply engrossed in Grandpa's description of the bar, the reason I got into trouble with the police. Not some active intent to ignore me. I still didn't like it, though–why would they, non-drinkers, be so interested in the bar? I must say that my bad experiences there really shaped my perception of it.

The next day, I grabbed the will and took it to school. I would show everybody and let them know about the library, and how important it was to our community!

As I went into my first class, World History, I thought about the different ways I could spread the news. Not only among my peers, but also to the teachers and adults. I could tell them casually during an assignment, or I could make a big deal about it and get them all hyped up about it.

As expected, Ms. Wentworth gave us an assignment at the end of class after her lesson. It was a relatively easy one, where you just had to match the civilization to its proper spot on the map. After finishing, I turned to the person behind me, Kenneth. He had also finished the assignment and was just sitting there, doing nothing.

"You know the bar, right?"

"What?" he responded.

"The one on Kern and Delano," I said.

"Oh," he replied, looking intrigued. "What about it?"

"Apparently, it was actually... a library!" I uttered the last part with a low voice and a grin.

The girl sitting in front me turned around.

"What was actually a library?" she asked. This was exactly what I wanted! The more people, the better.

"The bar," I responded.

"I had no idea!" the girl, Grace, said.

"That's interesting," Kenneth responded. "I've never been to a library."

"My grandpa said it used to be special to this place, and that the bar ruined our town. Also, I found a will from the bar owner's father that told him to keep it a library! And that means–"

The bell rang, and everyone dashed out the door. Unfortunately, I couldn't find another opportunity during the school day to tell anyone else about the library. I started walking home, slightly disappointed that I could only tell two people about the library. And they were kids, of all people, who couldn't do much to change anything. I could only hope Grace and Kenneth would talk about it–but all they'd talk about is video games and annoying teachers.

As I walked down the street, I saw the generic sign of the local general store. It read:

"Dingerman's! We Never Compromise on Quality!"

I immediately veered off of my path and started walking towards the general store. I pulled the handle of the door and was greeted by a sharp, raspy grate of the door's hinges. I saw a wrinkled, smiling face look up from behind the cashiers' table. It was Mr. Dingerman.

"Why, hello, son!" he said.

"Hi, Mr. Dingerman!"

"Do you need help finding anything?" he

asked. "We just got a new collection of fine soaps and shampoos! Interested?"

I chuckled and replied, "No thanks,"

Mr. Dingerman got up and said, "Hold on a second, Dan, I'll give you a tour of our fabulous soaps! I'll give them to you for cheap."

"But–"

"Hush, now, you'll be enchanted by them when you see them. They're my pride and joy as of now. We don't get these kinds of shipments every day, you know."

He guided me to the very back of the store, behind the aisles and rows. There was a large, green blanket covering something up, most likely the soap and shampoo display he had been talking about.

He grinned. "Are you ready?"

I nodded, and he lifted the cover to reveal a grandiloquent display of soap bars of every color. There were red ones, blue ones, pink ones, purple ones, yellow ones, and even multi-colored ones. The smell was overwhelming, but it really was quite a sight to see.

"Do you like it?" he asked, beaming.

"It's great!" I responded, despite the fact that I didn't know much about soaps, and I didn't have much of an interest to know more about them.

He picked a red one up and held it out to me. "Take this one, son, I'll give it to you at a discount!"

I reached into my pockets and found nothing. Lukas had all my change.

"I don't have any money on me right now, though," I said.

He frowned. "Oh, that's a shame. Maybe next time!"

He paused, and said, "So you just came here to take a look around?"

"Well, yes–er, no, you see–I actually wanted to tell you something interesting I discovered a while back. About the bar on Kern and Delano."

He sat down and immediately looked engrossed in the matter.

"Sit down, then," he said, beckoning to a seat

across from him. It was right next to the soap display. "Tell me."

"My grandpa told me that the bar was originally a library. It was a place where everyone could connect and relax. It was like a community center, apparently. Everyone was happy and content with the library. However, the library owner died and left it to his son, who turned it into a bar with the interest of profit. But in the will left by his father, it says to keep it a library!"

"Wait, how do you know about the will?"

"Uh... I got it."

He looked perplexed.

"What?"

I hesitantly took it out of my backpack and unfolded it. Now, he looked genuinely surprised.

"You actually got the will? How? Where?"

"I, uh, sneaked into the bar through the back, and took it from one of the locked cabinets by unscrewing the whole cabinet off." I said it with a hushed tone. While it sounded great if you wanted to boast about your adventures to other kids, it probably didn't sound too great in front of an adult.

He didn't say anything for a while, and then burst out laughing.

"I see your point. The library was supposed to stay up according to the will."

"Yes," I answered, eager to push my intrusion out of the conversation.

"So you want the library rebuilt? We would have to talk to the city officials about that."

"Yes, I wanted to tell everyone in this community about it, so the city could know that everyone wants the library to be rebuilt."

"I'm certainly not against it." he stated. "But I think you'll have to tell more people than me if you want it to gain traction," he added with a smile.

"Definitely. Well, thank you, Mr. Dingerman!"

"No problem, son. And don't forget about those soaps! Tell your mother! Tell your father! Tell your grandpa! Tell everyone at school! Tell everyone in the community while you tell them about the library!"

I laughed. "I surely will, sir!"

And with that, I opened the door and walked out.

CHAPTER 13: PAPER REFILL

Dan

It was cold outside, so I rushed back home quickly and went straight to my mother.

"Mom, I went to Dingerman's. To tell him about the library," I said.

She was sitting down on the couch with a cup of tea.

"What did he say?"

"He just said I need to tell more people," I responded.

"I agree. You need to be able to tell everyone about this if you want to make it big around here."

I sighed. "I was only barely able to tell two kids at school, and they probably didn't take it too seriously, given that the bell rang while I was telling them."

"I have an idea. You could put little pieces of paper around town with information about the library."

"Like advertisements?"

"Yes! They would be big and bold, and have to catch the public's attention well."

"I'll start making one, then! Then, we can go to the public copy machine in City Hall."

I went up to my room, filled with a renewed energy. I grabbed a piece of paper and laid it on my desk. I scoured the room for that box of markers I had. They used to be under my bed, but I had forgotten where I had placed them. After all, it had been months since I had been assigned a project that required them. I finally found the markers hiding in the corner of my dresser. I brought them over to my desk and just sat there for a while, thinking about what I could do.

An idea sprung into my head and I instantly started, grabbing the bright red marker. At the top, I wrote in large letters, "DID YOU KNOW?" I then took the black marker and started sketching a picture of the bar. It wasn't great, but it was an illustration that definitely spruced up the whole thing and was intended to catch the eye of the viewer. I drew a rectangle with two windows and a door between the two. And at the very top, I drew a sign. In blue ink, I wrote "Caddy's" in the sign with the best handwriting I could do it in. I took a black pen and started writing: "The Bar on Kern and Delano... was once a Library! The Library was a place where we could all bond and have good times. But the Bar is wrecking peoples' lives. Ask our city officials to TEAR DOWN the Bar and REBUILD the Library now!" I stared in dismay at how my penmanship had slowly deteriorated, but decided that as long as it was still legible, it was fine.

I went downstairs with the paper, and exclaimed, "Mom! I finished it! Can we go to the copier in town hall?"

"That quickly? Wow. I can drive you there," she said, getting up. I showed her the paper, which she quickly approved.

There was a rather long line for the copier machine today, about ten or so folks. They all looked about as frustrated as we were with the line. What made it worse was that each person seemed to be printing an infinitely-large number of papers.

"They must be printing the whole dictionary," I remarked quietly, which made my mom chuckle.

It was finally our turn. We stepped up and I put the paper under the printer. After pressing the appropriate buttons (which I noticed were covered in layers of sweat and grime from all the hands that had touched them), we waited for the papers to come out. But they didn't. There was an error message on the screen, reading, "Refill Paper".

"Oh, come on!" My mom exclaimed, putting her arms up in the air.

"I told you that they were printing the whole dictionary," I responded.

We asked a lady who was passing by–someone who worked there–if they had extra paper.

Paper refilled, we were finally able to get fifty copies of the flier, and went outside, where the sun was already about to set. We had brought a lot of nails, and a hammer, which I was holding.

"I think we can nail some of these to the telephone poles before it gets too dark," Mom remarked, looking for one. She took one of the nails in my hand and went over to one in front of town hall. She held the paper on the surface with her hand and put a nail to it. I then went and hammered it, securing it in place.

"It looks good against brown," she said.

"It does look nice," I replied, satisfied with my almost-professional creation.

We went around the town and stuck them to the telephone poles around the town. We strategically put them near places we knew a lot of people passed by, so that as many people as possible knew about it. We put them near the general store, near the post office, at almost every intersection, near the school, and even the bar. It soon became too dark to keep going, so we had to stop, despite still having six more. I was proud of our work, and couldn't wait to see the town's reaction as the days and weeks went on.

CHAPTER 14: YOUTHFUL ENTHUSIASM

City Clerk

As the clerk at the office in City Hall, I witnessed the ebb and flow of the town's daily activities. People came and went, using the public services we provided, and each day brought its own set of stories and interactions. But on that particular day, something caught my attention– a young boy and his mother with a sense of determination and purpose.

They entered the office with a sheet of paper in hand, their faces alive with anticipation. The boy seemed eager, his eyes shining with enthusiasm as he talked about a project he had undertaken. It was clear that this endeavor held great importance to him, and his mother listened attentively, nodding in agreement.

Curiosity piqued, I observed them closely as they discussed their plan. The boy held a vibrant paper, a homemade flier he had meticulously crafted to capture attention and convey his message. His passion for the cause shone through every stroke of his markers.

With their request to use the public copy machine, they joined the line that snaked its way through the office. Impatience hung in the air, a shared sentiment among those waiting. The copier seemed to be testing everyone's patience, and I couldn't help but smile at the boy's comment about printing the whole dictionary.

Finally, it was their turn, and I watched as they encountered an unexpected obstacle–a paper refill error. I found them paper as soon as I could, having anticipated the incident–when you're printing hundreds of fliers, you're going to need a refill. They obtained the copies they needed, ready to spread their message throughout the town.

I watched them leave City Hall, armed with their flyers and a bundle of nails. Their intention was clear–to make their cause known to as many people as possible. It was a simple act, yet it held the potential to ignite conversations and spark change within the community.

I couldn't help but feel a surge of admiration for their efforts. In a world often filled with apathy and indifference, witnessing such passion and determination brought a renewed sense of hope. This young boy and his mother were actively working to make a difference, believing in the

SAMUEL PARIGELA

power of their voices and the ability to create change. They had set something in motion.

CHAPTER 15: AGE OF EMPLOYMENT

Dan

I was coming back home from school one day, observing the fliers we had put on the telephone poles. On one of the poles, I saw another piece of paper under our flier. When I came closer, it seemed to be high quality material, not just a flimsy piece of paper. It was an advertisement for a summer job at the mayor's office. The ad read, "Teach Your Kids Responsibility and Integrity From a Young Age! Become a Page at the Mayor's Office this Summer! Applications Open, so DON'T WAIT–see the Reception at Town Hall for More Details!" Now this was interesting. Grandpa was talking about telling the city council members and the mayor about the library. Getting a summer job would just be fantastic, especially seeing that school ended in only a couple days at this point.

I went home and told my parents, saying, "Mom! Dad!"

"Dan, what is it?" responded my dad, and my mom also looked up at me.

"I saw an ad while coming back from school to be a page at the Mayor's office," I said, eagerly.

"Like some sort of internship?" Mom asked.

"Yes. It would be great, right?"

"For some pocket money?" Dad asked, grinning.

"Pocket money? Why, no! If I can get directly into the Mayor's office, I can tell him about the library and the will," I said, surprised my parents had forgotten about the library.

"Oh, I see," he said.

"That's actually a good idea," Mom said. "So, do you just go there and say you want to work at the mayor's office?"

"I guess," I responded. "The ad said applications are already open."

"I can take you over to Town Hall then," Dad offered.

"Then, let's go!" I said, and we got in the car.

We took a short trip over to Town Hall, where I had printed the fliers at its public copier machine.

We walked inside. It was majestic and lavish inside, with pillars and red carpets everywhere. For such a small and insignificant town, it sure was a lot. There were also a number of advertisements for the job I was seeking, except they were much larger, having been printed on banners.

There was an employee sitting behind a desk, near where we had entered. He was probably some sort of receptionist.

"Hello," he said, with a small smile.

"I would like to enroll my son as a page for the mayor's office," Dad said. "He saw an ad for it, and he's interested."

"Great! You can just sign up right here and select a date. You can write your address right next to it, along with your son's name and age," the receptionist answered, taking out a clipboard and a pen.

"Date? Address? For what, shifts?"

"Shifts?" He chuckled. "Why, it's a date for the interview. The address is required to send you the results, which should come in a day or two."

"There's an interview too? Wow," Dad responded, quite surprised, as he took the clipboard and pen from the receptionist.

He turned to me and asked, "Will tomorrow be good?"

"Sure," I responded.

"What's in the interview?" I asked the receptionist.

"Oh, it's a very simple process. Nothing too big. They just ask you about your work ethic, and about life, and a lot of easy questions. You don't have to prepare, as there won't be anything you have to study for."

"Okay," I responded, satisfied.

Dad handed him back the clipboard and pen, saying, "Thank you!"

"No problem! If you guys are coming tomorrow, our open slots are at 3:30 PM and 6 PM." He said. Looking at me, he continued, "And good luck tomorrow, young man!"

"Thanks!" I said, and we left.

I got home, and after finishing my homework, asked Dad, "Are you sure I don't need to do anything else for the interview?"

"Like what? Studying?"

"Yeah. I know he said that I don't need to... but, maybe I can still try to be as ready as possible? I can think of what to say about my work ethic."

Dad chuckled. "It's okay, Danny! I'm sure it won't be too difficult, especially if they're recruiting kids. Plus, I'm pretty sure it's supposed to be some sort of personality or character test. Just to see how you'll work if you get the job."

"Oh," I said, starting to understand what he meant. It was all making sense now. At least sort of. The "work ethic" part was making sense. But why would they want to know about my life? That seemed a bit extreme.

"Make sure you don't boast about anything. That's the last thing they would want. Don't try to make yourself seem too humble, either, though. You could really be seen as a liability at that point."

"Yes," I said, still thinking about what Dad said about it being a 'personality or character test'.

"You're really just thinking too hard about this, Dan. If you don't get the job, I'm sure there are plenty of other ways you can influence the mayor or the city council," Dad remarked, and got up to go to another room.

He was right. There were probably other ways for me to get the news to the Mayor's ears. Or at least the city council's ears. But to actually be in the Mayor's office and work there was a literal gold mine. It would be, by far, the easiest way to get to the Mayor. At this point, failure was not an option.

The following day, the only thing I could think about at school was my interview. It was the only thing that was on my mind. Everything else went through one ear and came out the other–the exact opposite of what teachers say to do.

After school, I went home and asked my mom if I needed to do anything else for the interview. Just for a second opinion.

"Why are you so worried?" she asked. "I'm sure you will do great. Besides, it's not a *real* job or anything! It'll be easy, trust me."

At 3:20, Mom and I left to go to Town Hall. She dropped me off at the entry, where I walked according to a bunch of signs placed leading to the interview room. There were a lot of other students there, some with their parents, some who had probably just walked alone or with a friend. I had completely forgotten. There would be other kids here, too! I started to panic. I never expected it to be a competition. Now that I think about it, it was dumb to not think there would be other candidates. That really only makes sense!

"Oh no," I whispered to myself, standing at the end of the line. Compared to other kids, there was no way I was in any way better than them. A lot of them were probably older than me. Some of them could've even had this job last summer!

"Well," I said to myself, sighing. "I guess I'll have to find another way to reach the mayor."

Kids went in and out relatively quickly. Having brought my watch, I timed one of the boys who went in–just five and a half minutes. The line moved quickly until it was my turn. I would go in and do my best. And if I did well, I would be chosen. If there were other people who were better than me (and I wasn't even completely sure what the interviewers would judge you by), then I would just have to find another way. And there were probably plenty of those. I stepped in, greeted by a small, cozy, windowless room. A soft, yellow chandelier at the top set a warm mood, with red carpeting forming the floor. The wallpaper in the room was red, with golden flowers rising from the floor and ending at the middle area of the wall. There was a table in the middle of two foldable chairs, one of which was occupied by the interviewer, a serious-looking, bald man with a small cluster of hairs on his chin. It almost looked like he shaved his beard but missed a sliver of it.

"Hi. I'm the secretary of the Mayor's Office. It's Dan, right?" he said in a deep–but not gruff–voice.

"Yes," I said, quietly.

"I'm just here to ask you a couple questions. Nothing too serious. So. How's school?"

"It's going well."

"How are your classmates? What do you think of them? Be honest. I'm not telling anyone."

"Truthfully, I respect them and admire them. And I have developed a kind of atmosphere where they tend to respect me, too." Perhaps not all of them, but... most of them, at least.

"Nice," he responded, looking down at his

papers. "How do you help others at school?"

"I help kids with their classwork while the teacher is busy with others. Sometimes even when I don't get to finish my own work."

"Really? That's great," he said, nodding.

He asked a couple more questions, not only about school, but about other things in life. Some of them weren't even necessarily related to the job I wanted or anything.

After a couple minutes of asking questions and writing stuff down on his paper, he let me go.

"That's it! Thank you! You'll get your results in the mail, within at least two days."

"Thank you, sir!" I responded, and left, glad it was finally over. Walking home, I realized that Dad was right–it was more of a test to see how I reacted and what I was like. Or as Dad said, some sort of personality or character test.

The next day, after school, I went to our mailbox before going home.

I opened it and found a couple papers. After sifting through them, I couldn't find anything

SAMUEL PARIGELA

about the mayor's office job.

I went inside, where Mom asked, "Did it come, yet?"

"No," I responded. "I suppose it'll just come tomorrow."

The next day, I stopped at the mailbox again. I opened it, and frantically started searching. After a few seconds of digging wildly, I finally found an envelope signed from Town Hall.

"Yes!" I exclaimed, loud enough for my mother to hear me from inside the house.

"What is it? Did it come?" she asked, coming outside.

"It did. Oh, I'm so nervous!"

We went inside and I carefully broke the seal on it. The first word: "Congratulations!"

"Wow!" Mom said, thrilled. "You got the job!"

I must say, I had relatively low expectations in respect to my prospects of getting the job. Out of all those kids, they chose me! That was crazy.

86

When Dad came back, I told him as well. Like Mom, he was pleasantly surprised.

"I knew you would do it! Fantastic job!" he said, hugging me.

I continued reading the paper. It said that I would have to come every day (except Sunday) from 8 AM to 4 PM. Until school ended, I could work from 3 PM to 7 PM. It seemed like a lot, but now that I got the job, there was no way I could say "no"! It also said that in order to accept it, one of my parents would have to sign it and it would have to be dropped off at the reception by a certain date. I must say, I had always thought that receptionists just answered phone calls and greeted visitors. They definitely did a lot more than that.

Mom signed the paper and we went to drop it off at the receptionist, who congratulated me upon seeing what the document was.

"Amazing! This isn't an opportunity everyone gets," he said, receiving the paper.

"Thank you," I replied, quietly, but internally extremely happy at my success.

CHAPTER 16: TICKET TO SUCCESS
Dan

Having woken up early, about an hour and a half before I would go to school, I was sitting in my room on my bed, looking outside. We had put some of the fliers on the trees in our neighborhood, as there weren't too many telephone poles around there. I saw a family walk by one of the trees we had put a flier on. There was a mom, a dad, and two little girls, both looking like they were maybe about three or four years old. They stopped by the flier for a bit and appeared to be reading it carefully. One of the girls pointed to the flier.

"Library," she said to her parents.

Her mom bent down and read the flier.

"The bar was supposed to be a library? You learn something new every day."

The dad commented, "This is pretty interesting. I never knew that, or even paid much attention to that old bar. It seems like it's been here forever."

"It couldn't hurt to have a library, I guess,"

the mom responded. "Plus, libraries are definitely more useful than bars. People can gain knowledge, rather than getting drunk the entire night."

At this point, I started feeling guilty that I was eavesdropping on a conversation that they didn't intend for me to listen to. However, I did find it interesting that first of all, someone actually paid attention to my flier. It was encouraging to see people actually take a good look at my flier. But I felt like I wanted a stronger reaction from them. Also, my new job at the Mayor's office would be pointless if he didn't know about the whole situation with the library. I didn't want to tell him too directly, or even too soon. I would probably panic, and tell him the wrong stuff, or maybe omit some details.

I raced out of my room and stopped on one of the middle steps on the stairs.

"Mom!" I yelled.

"Yes?" she responded, from across the room.

"How much does a billboard cost?"

"What?" She looked confused.

"One of those things you see on the highway, the big rectangular–"

"I know what a billboard is," she said, cutting me off. "But why do you want one? Those are quite expensive."

"Expensive?" I replied, disappointed to some degree. I must say, I had really forgotten that price was a factor here. "I mean, I feel like those fliers just aren't cutting it."

"What do you mean?" she responded, curious to know more.

"I feel like I need some sort of medium where I can provide a longer description. I realized that I had missed a couple details."

"Well, why were you asking for a billboard? In general, billboards need to actually be shorter than a flier, seeing that people can't exactly stop to read one. Unless it's rush hour, of course."

She had caught me there, I will admit.

"I guess... I didn't really think through that very well."

"It's okay," she said, smiling. "I'm pretty sure what you wrote on the flier was pretty long, no? If you want something longer, you'd have to get it in the newspaper or something."

"Yes! That's it!" I blurted out, almost before she finished her sentence.

"You want it in the newspaper? What would you write?"

"I would use what I wrote in the flier, except with a couple additions. It wouldn't be too long–think of it as more of an advertisement, except in the Opinion section. Also, the newspaper would allow us to reach out to more people, because practically everyone we know here reads the newspaper! Every person here will at least know about the library, and of those people there will at least be a couple people willing to stand up and do something, right?"

"Yeah, I guess. Maybe we can go to the newspaper's office today, after school. There are a couple papers around, so we'll have to pick one."

I went to school, arriving just on time to my first class. Ms. Wentworth was at the front of the class, talking about her day or whatever. She was reading a small piece of paper and talking about something she saw in the news. I blanked out pretty quickly, as she never had anything of value to talk about. Nothing she said was even that interesting.

Five minutes passed, ten minutes passed, fifteen minutes passed... yet she hadn't started the lesson yet. I groaned of boredom. She immediately turned around to grab a pen to start the lesson, so quickly that I was actually afraid she had heard my groan.

As she turned around, however, the paper in her hand slipped out and wafted away from her. It took twists and turns and went in circles for a short while, but its final resting spot was on the very corner of my desk. I turned around and took a good look at the rest of the class. All of them were somehow engrossed in whatever she was talking about. It didn't look like any of them had seen the paper leave her hand.

I grabbed the paper and put it on my desk, covering it with my hands on the sides, so that no one could see me reading it. It was a newspaper entry from *The Jeffrey Heights Transcript* about the various pests that destroy crops in our town. Jeffrey Heights was a community located within our town. It was rather small, but it was known for being safe and looked cleaner than a lot of the other places near our town. That being said, for some reason, everyone in town–whether they lived in Jeffrey Heights or not–received *The Jeffrey Heights Transcript*.

On the back of the paper was an

advertisement for the newspaper itself. It read, "Have something to say? Get your article in the MOST WIDELY READ NEWSPAPER in Town!" Under it was the address of the newspaper's office and its phone number. Maybe this was it–what luck! I could put my story about the library right here, in *The Jeffrey Heights Transcript*! I folded the paper and kept it in my pocket until school let out.

After school, I went straight to my mom.

"Mom, I found something!"

"What is it?" she asked.

"I found the newspaper we should choose," I said, holding the paper up.

"Oh, it's The Transcript! Very popular around here. Where did you get that piece of paper?"

"Uh, at school," I responded, trying to avoid the fact that it was technically not mine, but the teacher's...

"Where in school did you get it?" She prodded me further.

"It was... on my desk."

She laughed, half of her not believing the fact that someone had just left it there on *my* desk.

"Well, I guess we can go, then," she said, glancing at the clock.

We hopped in the car and took a short drive over to the newspaper office which was in Jeffrey Heights, of course. I had always heard good things about the place, but it was better than I had imagined. The roads were in good shape, unlike the various cracks in the roads we had. The trees and grass were trimmed to perfection.

The office was a four-story building built very extravagantly. It was grand and stately, incorporating the styles of ancient Greece in its architecture. We stepped out of our car and headed into the lobby. The lobby had a floor that appeared to be made out of marble, with an elegant, green carpet covering it. There was a receptionist waiting for us behind the counter.

"Hi!" she said. "How can I help you two today?"

"Hello! We're looking to inquire about putting a story in the newspaper," Mom responded.

"You can go see our Editor-in-chief in room 103, just down that hallway," she said, pointing to a corridor behind us.

"Thanks," my mom said, and we started walking down the hallway, looking for room 103.

We found it and looked through the window. It was a small office room, with a large computer, much like the one we had at home, except bigger. There was also a gigantic stack of papers on his desk.

Mom knocked on the door, to which he got up and opened it.

"Hello," he said. "Take a seat. I'm Brad Willington, Editor-in-chief here at The Transcript."

"Hi," my mom said. "I'm Michelle, and this is my son Dan."

"Nice to meet you!" he said, shaking both of our hands. "What brings you two here today?"

"I just wanted to inquire about the submissions process here for the Opinion section."

"It's quite simple. All you need to do is

email us a file of the submission."

"Could you please tell me the email?"

"Oh!" he exclaimed. "Of course. You know, once we get a website up and running, we'll be able to put the email up there." He leaned in closer and whispered, "Our goal is to become the first private company in town with a website!"

He took a Post-It note and wrote the email down for us.

"Here you go," he said. "Good luck!"

"Thank you so much!" my mom said, and we exited the building.

We went home and I turned our computer on. I grabbed the flier and opened the word processing tool. I began copying the flier, word for word. However, I started expanding on *why* the bar was as destructive as I claimed it was. I typed as fast as I could, while making sure I had hit all the right points and didn't miss anything. Also, I talked about the will. At the end of it, I had achieved a decent four hundred word paragraph. And my wrists hurt really bad.

I went downstairs and tiredly said, "Mom, I

finished."

"That fast?"

"Yep. I wrote really fast!"

She asked me to show her what I had written, so I showed her. I specifically pointed out where I changed things, since most of it was from the flier, which she had already approved of before.

"Yes, I think this is good. You can go ahead and email it to the newspaper. You have the sticky note, right?"

"Yes," I said, holding it up.

I emailed my article to the newspaper, and had to hope for the best.

Later in the evening the next day, I went and checked the email on the computer.

"Did they respond, yet?" Mom asked from downstairs.

"No," I said.

"Don't worry, just be patient. I suppose you can't really expect them to give you a reply in one day."

Days passed, and there was still no response. Soon it had gone to the back of my mind, as I started to think less and less about it.

One day, however, I received an email from the newspaper:

Dear Dan,

Your submission has been accepted and will be published next week on Wednesday. Make sure to look out for it then!

Regards,
Brad Willington
Editor-in-chief, *The Jeffrey Heights Transcript*

I raced downstairs, grinning at my good luck. First, I got a job at the mayor's office, and next, my submission was accepted at The Transcript!

"Mom! They responded! They said they would publish it next week on Wednesday!"

"Really? That's great!" she said happily.

On Wednesday at the Mayor's office, I started

the day collecting mail. I also noticed a copy of The Transcript. Flipping through it, I stopped at the opinion section when I saw my piece, about the library and the will. As a matter of fact, I had the will in my backpack, which I took to my job every day.

I went into his office, where he was drinking coffee and typing something up on his computer.

"Hi, sir," I said, bringing in the mail.

"Morning, Dan," he replied, focused on what he was typing up.

I went and put the envelopes and other various things sent in the mail on his desk. However, I made sure to put the newspaper on top of the pile. He wasn't looking. I pushed it slightly to make it fall, and then caught it, to make it look like the newspaper had slipped off. It was just one of my attempts to get his attention. Unfortunately, it was unsuccessful. I didn't want to put a show in front of him, so I left, quite disappointed that he didn't bother to look up, even a teeny bit.

CHAPTER 17: WHY THE LONG FACE?

Dan

As the days went on, I kept waiting for him to say something, just something, about the library or about the will. But the mayor never said anything. I don't think he even read the newspaper. If he didn't read the newspaper, this job was nothing more than a waste of time for me! It was all very discouraging.

One day, feeling disheartened, I decided to go the extra mile and fetch him a cup of coffee in the morning. I slowly trudged over to the coffee pot, the weight of my disappointment dragging me down. I poured some coffee into a cup, adding sweetener and a bit of cream with a lackluster motion. With the cup in hand, I dragged myself over to his desk and gave him the coffee mug. Again, he just nodded in acknowledgement without a word.

The next day, I arrived at work carrying a heavy cloud of sadness, not realizing how much it showed on my face. I went about my usual tasks, getting the mail, making his coffee (by this time, I had learned how much he loved his coffee), and more. He had just printed something and asked me to retrieve it from the copier machine, which was different from the public one. This one was reserved particularly for the mayor and other staff.

As I went about my duties, I couldn't help but feel increasingly worried about whether the newspaper would reach him. It seemed like every minute, more papers would come piling on top, obscuring the newspaper from his view. Now, there was only a small, barely visible portion of the paper sticking out. Dejected, I slouched my way to his desk, looking at the ground and completely absorbed in my uneasiness, almost oblivious to the fact that I was walking towards the mayor.

"What's wrong, Dan?" the mayor asked, catching me off guard. I froze up, realizing that I hadn't noticed him eyeing me carefully, trying to decrypt the code of my expression that was gazing downwards.

I immediately attempted to look more cheerful and said, "Oh, nothing is wrong, Mr. Mayor."

"I can see that you're upset about something, Dan," he said softly, still trying to interpret the look in my eyes. "If it's something you aren't comfortable telling me about, it's okay."

My heart raced. This was my chance, my opening. If I said I didn't want to tell him, I would be wasting multiple hours every day.

"Actually, I, uh, sort of have something I specifically wanted to tell you about," I mustered the courage to speak up.

He looked even more interested, leaning forward in his chair. "Is that so? Go ahead, go ahead. And feel free to take a seat."

I pulled out the chair across from him and sat down, taking a deep breath. "Have you seen the story about the library in the newspaper?"

"No," he answered, to my dismay. "Usually, I don't get a whole lot of time to read the newspaper as I'm wrapped up in my mayoral duties most of the time. If anything particularly important or eye-catching comes up, my staff will inform me about it. Or, if I'm not too busy, I can take the time to read it myself, whether it be on a break or at home. That's enough of me talking, anyway," he chuckled. Reaching for the newspaper amongst his stack of papers, he asked, "Could you find the article you're talking about and show me, please?"

"Definitely," I responded, my hopes rising. I

quickly flipped two pages to the opinion section. "Here it is," I said, pointing to it.

He put on his reading glasses and began skimming through the article, his brows furrowing in concentration. Finally, he looked up at me and said, "I see, I see... First of all, who wrote this? It's excellent."

"You see, I did, uh..." I started, my voice trailing off.

"You're saying that you wrote this?" he interrupted, his eyes widening.

"Yes," I said timidly, feeling shy.

"I knew it from the beginning. You're quite a brilliant young man!" he exclaimed, patting me on the back. "So, you're saying here that you want the bar replaced with a library?"

"Exactly. I highlighted a couple of points as to why the bar must be shut down. Not only that, but also why a library must be built, and was supposed to be there all along."

He nodded in understanding. "I get it. I have received a whole lot of reports about alcohol-related crimes, and sometimes even general public drunkenness. Many times, these are tied into the bar you are talking about. I understand why a library could benefit a community. When I was growing up, I remember a couple of memories of the library. And I will say, it was a great place," he said, his voice filled with nostalgia. "I saw that it was a burden to manage, however," he added, laughing. "But I also saw that the folks in charge there really loved doing it."

"There's also the will," I added, seizing the opportunity to share more information.

"The last will? Of the library's owner?" he inquired, intrigued.

"Yes, the will specifically stated that the library had to remain a library. That implies that the bar isn't supposed to exist and the library was never supposed to be demolished in the first place."

"How do you know about all this?" he asked, curiosity evident in his voice.

"My grandfather told me, sir."

"Okay. But how do you know what the will says?"

"I, uh, obtained it," I confessed, feeling a mix

of guilt and determination.

"Obtained it? How, exactly?" he questioned, raising an eyebrow.

"Well, so, I basically sneaked into the back of the bar and stumbled upon a piece of paper that happened to be the will," I explained, feeling slightly apprehensive about revealing my methods.

He frowned slightly, perhaps a hint of disapproval, when he realized that I had technically engaged in criminal activity. "I see. If you want the bar replaced by the library... Well, I hate to say it, but I'm sure you must be aware that there are a lot of people who won't take the prospect of the bar being destroyed very lightly."

"Yes," I said, nodding my head. "I've seen tens of people in line outside that place. But you, Mr. Mayor, yourself, said that you have received a lot of reports of alcohol-related crimes. Not only would destroying the bar make this town a better place, but building the library up again would make this town a community again. Grandpa was talking about how when the library was around, everyone felt like family. I'm sure there are more people in this town who would prefer that over having a bar open."

"I will look into it considerably," he said, his voice thoughtful. "Thank you so much for bringing this to my attention, Dan. You have only been here for a short period of time, but I recognized you for being a different, deeper, more thoughtful kid."

"Thank you, sir," I said, feeling a swell of pride.

"Have a good evening, Dan," he said, escorting me out the door.

"You too, Mr. Mayor," I replied, walking away with a newfound sense of hope.

As I got up out of my chair, I noticed something behind the mayor. Right behind him was a small photo with a few people in it. Underneath it were scrawled the words, "The Caddies." Strange.

CHAPTER 18: A PARTICULAR REFERENDUM

Dan

The next day, I went to work feeling content and satisfied. I had managed to successfully show the mayor what I was concerned about. Now, the only thing I had to worry about was if he was actually going to do anything about it. I started the day making his coffee, going over to the coffee pot and pouring some.

I went to hand it over to him, and he said, "Thank you, Dan."

"No problem," I replied. But as I turned to leave, he called me back.

"Wait, Dan."

"Yes?" I responded, turning back.

"I was thinking about what we could do to tear down this bar and to rebuild the library. And I got an idea. We would need the consent of the people to do anything as tremendous as this. So, we would have to hold a referendum."

"Okay," I said. "When would we have it?"

"I think I'll send out the referendum next week."

"Thank you, Mr. Mayor!" I exclaimed.

Next week, at work, the Mayor called me over again.

"The referendum for the library is out. People are at the ballot box, making their vote."

"I had actually put out a couple fliers on the telephone lines. I suppose those can now act as advertisements."

"Yes. I am definitely sure that the majority of people would take the library over the bar any day."

After work, I went home and told Mom that we needed to make more fliers, this time with the intention of getting people to vote for the library and against the bar.

"I'm going to make another flier," I said to her. "To tell people to vote for the library."

"Okay. When you're done we can go and get them printed."

I included less stuff on this version of the flier. I only explained that the bar is destructive while the library is a center of learning and bonding. Taking up the most space on the front page was a huge box that said, "Vote for the Library!" because that was the main, take-home message. Plus, voting for a library over a bar seemed like a relatively easy decision.

We went over to the copier machine in Town Hall and got a couple printed. This time, I taped them to places with more traffic, as there aren't any telephone poles right in the middle of shopping centers or malls, where a lot of people go. While the weather was likely to sweep the papers off if I taped them, the results would likely come in a couple days, so I wasn't too concerned about them falling off.

I went around these shopping centers and taped them as well as I could. I didn't have any sort of high quality tape or anything like that, so I used a lot of tape per flier.

On Wednesday, I got the newspaper along with other mail on my shift in the Mayor's office. The front page declared that the results for the referendum weren't out yet. I kept reading through the newspaper, until I found a peculiar piece in the Opinion section. The title read, "Why This New Referendum is Bogus. And Why You Shouldn't Vote For It." What? I continued scanning through the article. "The bar has always been a vital part of our society. Many past mayors and important city leaders have used this place as a way to pass time, to get away from the struggles of their busy lives, and most importantly, to have fun.

Today, it's a place for everyone to come and unwind. Everyone above a certain age, of course!" it said. But the bar was also linked to numerous crimes, according to the mayor. And that's not 'fun'. It also read, "It will be impossible for this to pass, seeing that this will almost certainly mean a tax hike for something that most people probably never wanted." Who even wrote this? I looked closer, only to find that the owner of the bar, Willis, was the one who wrote it.

I showed the article to the mayor, confounded.

"Well, Dan, it really only makes sense for him to attack this legislation. It directly endangers his business, the bar. He is trying to rally support against this bill."

"I'm sure the bar-goers will vote against it," I commented.

"Of course they will. That's pretty much a given."

"I put out more fliers today, except I made them to be geared towards this particular referendum."

"That's good. All we can do now is hope for the best. And I'm pretty sure it will happen."

CHAPTER 19: DON'T WORRY ABOUT IT!

Dan

The next day at the mayor's office, he called me over.

"So, Dan. I was thinking about the will. Could you possibly show it to me, one day?"

"The will? Why, of course! In fact, I have it with me right now!"

"You have the will?"

"I have it in my backpack."

He looked confused. "Do you carry it with you all the time?"

"No, I just knew that you'd probably ask."

"Okay, then. Good. Bring it over here, and I'll take a look at it."

I got the will out of my backpack and showed it to him.

"Wow," he said, surprised. "I will be honest, I really didn't expect to just get the whole will, as it is. So, you said you got it from the back of the bar?"

"Yes, I did." I always got a little edgy when anyone asked me about my visit to the back of the bar.

"So, show me where it talks about the library."

I went over to that part and pointed to it. It was as clear as day, not some blurry, misguided interpretation of mine.

"Oh. It's as clear as day, not some interpretation of yours," he said.

"Exactly. The one who wrote this will, Mr. Liam Caddel, made it as obvious as he could that he wanted the library to stay. Frankly, even if the library was still there but the bar was built separately, things would probably be fine."

"I'll tell you what, Dan: if the library was around, there would be no bar. The library was just a never-ending pit of learning and wisdom, and not only that, it was a place where friendships were built and never torn apart. Back when the

113

SAMUEL PARIGELA

library *was* still up, there was no time for other distractions like bars and pubs, and that sort."

I stayed silent; he had a good point there.

The mayor broke the silence, saying, "I'll talk to the bar owner about this privately, just to get his side of the story as well. While I definitely support the library's construction, I just want to get both sides of this matter, as all the evidence I have so far is pretty one-sided."

"I mean, the referendum is already out, right?" I said.

"I just want to check," he said. "Also, I would like to try to get him to see from the town's perspective, and to understand the negative effects of the bar and the positive effects of a library.

The next day, the mayor's doors were closed, as he was talking to the bar owner, Willis. It was all too interesting. Could "The Caddies" refer to the Caddels? Giving it a second thought, I decided not. "The Caddies" probably referred to the last name Caddy, or even just Caddie. Making a connection to the Caddel family seemed a bit wrong on my part. Never safe to assume. Although it seemed awfully similar.

114

Since the office doors were closed, I was forced to send mail and other papers in through a small slit next to the door that fed into a bin where the mayor could collect them and put them on his desk.

The little meeting between the mayor and Willis was over pretty quickly. I tried to listen through the aforementioned slit, but they were talking very quietly.

After Willis left, I went into the Mayor's office to ask him what Willis said to him.

"What did he say?"

With a weak chuckle, he said, "Well, I asked him straight on about the library. I didn't try to hide it by talking about other things at the beginning, because he knew that the reason for this meeting was the library. Why else would I have him come over, anyway?"

"What did he say about the library and taking down the bar?"

"As you might guess, he received it quite negatively. Very negatively, in fact. He kept talking about taxpayers' wallets being squeezed for something they probably didn't believe too much in. I just told him that we would see what the public thought once the referendum results came out. He was talking about the positive effects of the bar, and how it was something that let people relax, and the only place in town where people could find some sort of refuge from the business of work. I said that the library could also do that. People could talk to other people and relax that way, instead of promoting our town's already bad alcohol problem. And that was pretty much it. Of course, he expanded on his points a lot, and I expanded on mine, but that was just a shorter, summarized version of it."

"Okay. So once the referendum results come out, if people say yes to rebuilding the library... will you do it?"

"Why, of course! That's the point of a referendum. In fact, I actually asked the city council members about giving the referendum to the people, and they all voted yes. So we would have approval for the project on multiple levels."

"How soon would you do it?"

He smiled. "Whenever we get the materials and equipment. Don't worry too much about it, okay?"

I nodded. But how could I not? It was all I could think of!

CHAPTER 20: VICTORY

Dan

On Wednesday, I went to work, made the Mayor's coffee, and ran out to collect the mail from the lobby. It was here! I took a look at my watch. 8:18 AM. Usually the newspaper came at 8:30 or even 9. The front page read, "Townspeople Overwhelmingly Support Library In Referendum". Wow! Was it true? I read further. Apparently 89% voted for the library, while 11% voted against it.

I ran into the Mayor's office, elated and bursting with excitement.

"Mr. Mayor, did you hear the news? Did you hear the news?"

He grinned. "Why, yes, I most certainly did!"

"Isn't it great!"

"Of course!"

"Will you start building it?" I asked eagerly.

"I already ordered all the materials, and all the construction equipment is getting ready! Many people are donating to the cause as well!"

I continued reading the paper, and even kept reading past the article about the library. I soon stumbled on another article by Willis. It was titled, "The Library is Just Another Way to Take Your Money." The article went on to describe how the library would increase the taxes for something that was "completely unnecessary". Also, I noticed a reference to *my* article, saying that it was ironic that my article was published in a newspaper from one of the most lavish areas of the town.

It was essentially attacking my claims about crime caused by the bar by making it look like I knew nothing about crime since I published my article in a newspaper that was based in a wealthier location where there was little to no crime at all. But he was faulty in that surmise, because I *didn't* live in Jeffrey Heights. The newspaper went on to talk about all the jobs the bar created. However, in the long run, it had a negative impact on the community. At first, I wanted to publish an article countering his, but I didn't want to start something with him, so I decided not to.

Within a week, cranes with wrecking balls, excavators, and trucks showed up at the bar. I was watching with my parents a couple hundred feet away. We watched as hit by hit, the bar came tumbling down. Everything on the inside had been dismantled and taken away, so now, the only work left was to destroy the bar. The wrecking ball was huge, and probably weighed a ton, too. It was loud, and it was frankly painful to see something destroyed in such a manner. But it was a result of my work. And something to feel proud of.

Days passed, and me and my family went out for a walk to see the state of the bar. We were able to watch as a truck carried away the last load of debris and disappeared into the distance.

"Wow," Grandpa commented. "That took a lot less time than I had expected it to. I guess those wrecking balls really pack quite the punch!"

The next day, as I was walking home from work on a longer-than-usual day over at the mayor's office, I took a detour to pass by the construction site to see how things were going there. The foundations had been laid, and I could see metal beams standing vertically in the foundations. I sat down on a bench to watch the progress happen. To my dismay, however, all the workers had already left. I took a look at the huge trucks and cranes. They were so huge, I wondered how they had even got them here. As I stood up to leave, I noticed a couple people wearing dark clothes. Were they the construction workers? All the construction workers I had seen wore bright, orange vests and helmets. Plus, these people were sneaking around the property, looking suspicious. This, now, confirmed that they definitely were not construction workers. So what could they possibly be doing here?

I could hear them whispering to each other, but I couldn't make out the actual words they were saying. All of a sudden, one of them grabbed a beam. Then another one did. Then all of them were holding some of the beams. I was utterly confused. But what they did next was a real shocker. They all plucked them out of the ground and threw them every which way. Some of them banged against other poles, causing those to fall, too. One of the people took a box of nails and scattered them all on the foundations. Another took a can of paint also at the scene and poured it in. The others kicked wrenches and other tools on top of the whole mess. And they managed to spread it all over the entire site, which was quite large. Finally, they knocked a Porta-Potty down and scrambled. Those people were obviously up to no good! I would have said something, but I didn't want to get myself in trouble, so I stayed quiet.

As I went to work the next day, I went the long route again to see the site, and if the workers had fixed it yet. Unfortunately, they hadn't. It was sad to see the workers just shaking their heads at what had happened. Who could've done it? Who would purposefully try to obstruct the completion of the library? It was all absurd, really.

At the Mayor's office, I told him what I saw.

"I saw a couple people wearing dark clothes last night, and they were wrecking the whole place, essentially," I said.

"Yeah," he replied, sighing. "I got the report this morning that something happened to the site. But you're the first person I'm hearing who's actually seen it happen."

"I just took a detour when going home yesterday to see how the library is coming along so far, and as I was about to leave, a couple people–maybe four or five of them–started causing havoc."

"I think I know who's behind this. And I'm sure you do, too," he remarked.

"Who?"

"You know who," he said, smiling.

"Oh. Wait. It's the bar owner?"

"I'm positive," he said.

"Really? I never had a good impression of him, but that would practically be vandalism, right?"

"He's desperate, what can I say?"

I went straight home, and told Mom.

"I saw a couple people vandalizing the construction site, and the Mayor thinks the bar owner sent them to do it."

"That's terrible!" she said. "What can the city do about it?"

"I don't know, really. All I can do is hope that whoever is responsible for this stops what they're doing."

Weeks passed. Progress on the library continued. In other words, things seemed to be going well. The basic form of the library was starting to take shape now. The walls were already up, and most of the construction happening now was on the inside.

I went to the library to watch it as it evolved

SAMUEL PARIGELA

every day after work. One dark evening I was walking home, and as I reached Kern and Delano, I heard a "*CRASH!*" Startled, I leaped backwards, looking around to see what caused the noise. My eyes soon focused on a heap of rubble by the side of the building. I moved to another spot to get a better angle at it. It was a pile of broken bricks. There was a huge gap in one of the first-floor walls. There was another "*CRASH!*" This time, it came from the other side. I scurried in the direction of the second noise, and saw that that wall had been damaged, too. And in the corner of my eye, I saw the same group of darkly-clothed people! Except this time, they had sledgehammers. So the reason they hadn't come back for so long was so that they could cause damage when it was almost done?

Of course, I told the Mayor about this the very next day. He assigned some of the local law enforcement members to serve as security during both the day and the night. Now, the work on the library could go on without any interruptions.

I had come to the site almost every day, and watched the library go from a skeleton to a building. Every day, multiple trucks went to and fro the construction site, each with different materials. It almost seemed like magic, the way it went from a couple feeble beams to a building that was now two stories high and looked magnificent. It was made of reddish-orange colored bricks, with a dark brown door and a palatial spire plated with gold at the very top. It was majestic.

At this time, the Mayor announced The Library Foundation, similar to the one Grandpa talked about. It was like a dream come true. In fact, it was what I was waiting for, even more than the library. The library was really just a building. But the Foundation was what brought people together and made it the special place that it was all those years ago.

The Mayor called me over at work and said, "I'm pleased to announce that we're planning on opening the library to the public next week on Tuesday!"

"That's amazing!" I replied, delighted.

"There will be a ribbon-cutting ceremony, and all that fun stuff."

I couldn't wait till next week. I had waited so long already, so a week, in theory, shouldn't seem too long. But it felt like forever.

Six days later, I was walking home from work and I went by the library to take one last glance at it before it opened. It was a masterpiece in all of its beauty and splendor. Even at night, the golden spire twinkled and gleamed in the moonlight.

CHAPTER 21: DREAM COME TRUE

Dan

The ribbon-cutting ceremony was scheduled to commence in one hour. We had received a shipment of a couple hundred books from bookstores and individuals. However modest of a number, it was still something to get us started. And for the rest of the month, people and businesses were encouraged to donate books–a book drive had been set up to the side, where people could drop off their books. The 'book drive' was really just a pickup truck with a sign taped to it, but it would work just fine.

Instead of working in the office today, the Mayor instructed me to go and help set up chairs, the podium, and tie the ribbon, which was a shiny red. I double-checked to make sure everything was proper–I made sure every row of chairs had the same number. I made sure that the podium wasn't too far off to the side, but not way out there. I fixed a banner that was slightly tilted. Slightly, but still noticeably. In other words, everything was ready. Now we just had to wait for the people to come.

And they did, in the hundreds, most of them carrying armfuls of books they wanted to donate. Among them were my parents. By the time everyone came, we had run out of chairs. People were sitting on the ground, leaning against the banners (as I looked on with dismay), or just standing in the corner. Books were falling out of the truck bed–it was so full–we had to stuff books inside the truck. About a half hour passed until the Mayor came and gave a short speech. He thanked all the people who helped make the library possible, and all the construction workers who made the plan a reality.

"...and I would especially like to thank Dan, the fine young man who came up with this concept, this beautiful idea that I am sure generations will remember him for."

He pointed towards me, as I melted in my own seat. Everyone had turned to look at me. I was unsettled by all the eyes that fixated on me, though most were warm looks, glowing smiles, and parents ready to tell their children "what a good kid he is, why can't you be like him". He then welcomed the newfound chair of the Library Foundation, a person called Leonard Strellis. Mr. Strellis seemed like a laid-back, thoughtful person, who introduced himself and then gave a brief history of the old library. I started liking him more, as it sounded like he was using the same talking points I used when talking about the old library. He mentioned the sense of community there was, and how everyone knew each other because of it. He did the usual thing with the thanking, thanking the city, thanking the workers, thanking 'Jerry' also known as Mr. Mayor, thanking me (thank goodness the same amount of staring didn't happen again), and pretty much thanking everyone who had anything to do with the project.

The time came for the ribbon to be cut. It gleamed, red and bright, in the sun. The Foundation members stood behind the ribbon and smiled for the cameras (one of them operated by my dad) as the Mayor cut the ribbon with a ridiculously large pair of scissors. Everyone stood up and applauded. I guess applause at a time like this is normal, ordinary, even obligatory. But when they all stood and clapped, I realized that they were clapping for the library which was the direct result of me getting the mayor to build it. In a way, they were clapping for me. It was like a standing ovation.

The large, brown doors swung wide open, and the library was officially accessible. All the people rushed inside, and quickly swarmed into the lobby. The hundred-or-so books which we already had were brought inside, on a wagon. The Mayor graciously gave me the honor of checking out the first book.

My options were limited. Most of the books were academic or scientific–everything from a Precalculus textbook to *The Layman's Guide to Clinical Ophthalmology (9th edition)*. A few novels were scattered through the pile, though I found that most of them were copies of the same book, and there were a total of three *different* novels in that pile. It was here that I realized everyone's eyes were on me, and I really needed to hurry up if I didn't want to keep everyone waiting. I quickly grabbed a *Merriam-Webster's Dictionary*, thinking that it was apt to be the first book checked out at the library. With the ceremonial part of the ceremony done, everyone else started checking out books as well. The checking-out was mostly symbolic, as I'm sure half the people there would have no need of an Accounting handbook or the seventh volume of a series on Psychology (we didn't have any of the other volumes unfortunately).

The book drive lasted for two weeks. It was the same brown truck that we had put out during the ceremony, except it had a tent over it, to protect from potential rain (though very unlikely) and the sun, especially. The Foundation did practically exactly what Grandpa said they did back then–there were brunches, book readings, speakers called in from other towns and universities, and more. Personally, I loved it. And my parents enjoyed it too. I felt like we had gotten closer together as a community. *This* is what I had signed up for when I devoted myself to building the library, somehow. It was more than just a building–something Willis didn't understand. And the public liked it too. We had to expand the parking to fit more cars when there was a special event.

Soon enough, a small café popped up. It was on the second floor, and though it occupied a rather small space in the corner, the smell of coffee wafted throughout the floor and halfway down the stairs. It was perfect. People could drink coffee and read books. In fact, I went to the café a lot myself.

After the two weeks, I decided to get some books from the truck.

"Mr. Mayor!" I ran through the crowd to the space behind the checkout area, where the mayor was. He was talking to the other Foundation members, but paused to look at me.

"Hey, Dan, what's up?"

"Would it be okay if I got the books from the truck?"

"Uh, okay... he said, trying to look through the library's front windows across the hundreds of

SAMUEL PARIGELA

heads. "I don't see the truck from here. It's probably fine, you don't need to go."

"I'll go anyway," I said, smiling. The mayor looked away.

I scurried through the crowd, trying to get to the door, when I saw a familiar face.

"Dan," he said, slightly smiling.

Oh. Oh no. I had totally forgotten! The project! I just... never submitted anything!

"Uh, I– I'm sorry, Mr. Dengel, I was working on it, just with the library and all–"

"Oh, it's okay! What you've done here–" he said, pausing to make a sweeping gesture with his hand, showing the entire interior of the library. "– is more important than any project. While I usually say getting distracted is the last thing you want to do, I can make an exception. You don't have to do it, Dan–either way, I noticed you working hard during class doing research and typing up articles," he said, his other hand on my shoulder.

I was relieved. "Thank you so much, Mr. Dengel. It means a lot to me," I said quickly, and rushed out the door.

CHAPTER 22: TEMPTATION
Grandpa

From where I stood across the street, I watched the hullabaloo unfold. The old bar had turned into a library, and the whole town was havin' a grand old time, patting themselves on the back like they just discovered fire. Folks were buzzing with excitement, celebrating like there was no tomorrow. But deep down, a sneaky doubt started creepin' up on me, like an itch I couldn't scratch.

Was all the trouble of turnin' that bar into a library really worth it? My mind wandered back to the good ol' days when my parents couldn't resist the sweet poison of alcohol. It tore 'em apart, chewed 'em up, and spat 'em out. I worked my hardest to stay far away from that rotgut, but now, with the bar gone, it had this weird pull on me. It was like the forbidden fruit, temptin' me to take a bite.

I thought about Ma and Pa. When they were guzzlin' that devil's brew, they weren't fit to tie their own shoelaces, let alone take care of a family. I can still hear their slurred words, their broken promises floatin' in the air like shattered glass. But in the midst of all that chaos, I gotta admit, there were moments when that booze seemed like the only thing that could soothe their frayed nerves. It was a double-edged blade, cuttin' deep but also offerin' a false sense of relief.

As the town folks cheered and raised a glass, I couldn't help feelin' a twinge of envy. While they were celebratin' the birth of that fancy library, I was wrestlin' with my own demons. The urge to taste that forbidden drink kept growin', gnawin' at my willpower like a hungry dog on a bone.

In the midst of all the hoopla, my eyes settled on young Dan, runnin' around like a jackrabbit on a sugar high. He was full of life and curiosity. But as the crowd gathered for the ribbon-cutting, my mind kept wanderin' back to that old bar. It's like its closure only made its grip on me stronger, whisperin' that one little drink wouldn't hurt. It dangled promises of a quick getaway, a momentary escape.

But just as the big moment arrived and they snipped that ribbon, a flash of clarity hit me square in the gut. I'd fought tooth and nail, held my ground, to let some damn drink pull me under now would be a betrayal of everythin' I stood for. It'd be a slap in the face to Ma and Pa and a betrayal to myself. Strength ain't found in givin' in to temptation. But was I strong enough?

I took a deep breath and turned my back on the celebration.

CHAPTER 23: BETRAYAL
Dan

I was greeted by warm air and an equally pleasant sun, seemingly less oppressive than usual. What wasn't as pleasant, however, was the fact that I couldn't see the truck either. I picked up my pace, and went from a walk to a jog as I frantically searched for where the truck could've gone. The library had a sizable parking lot, yet it still wasn't enough for the hundreds of cars, some of which were forced to park across the street. And apparently some folks decided to just roll their cars into the grass next to the lot. I went up and down the rows of cars, searching for that one brown truck, and while it may sound like a difficult job, it really wasn't, as the truck wouldn't be hard to spot with all those books in the back. I was at it for about 20 seconds when I spotted something blinking from the corner of my eye.

I looked up and lo, and behold, there was the pickup truck I was looking for! The same pile of books in the truck bed. What was odd was that it wasn't in a parking space; rather, it was on the road, on the way out. The engine seemed to be... on? The tailights glowed red, the blinkers flashing orange, and if I listened close enough, the hum of the engine could be heard.

The car itself wasn't moving, but that appeared to be the result of traffic making it impossible for it to exit the parking lot.

I raced across the lot to the big doors and flung them open. My eyes darted around searching for the Mayor, and I spotted him in the corner talking to Mr. Strellis.

"Mr. Mayor, someone is taking the truck!" I exclaimed.

"One of the foundation members probably moved it, Dan. I'll be there, just give me a second," he replied, and went back to his conversation.

"But–" I saw he didn't want me making a big deal about it, so I spun on my heel and ran back.

The truck was still at the stop sign about to exit the parking lot, but the traffic was just beginning to die down. Whoever was driving the truck would soon escape, and then there would be no hope. I had to do something. I looked for anything to stop them, anything that could at least slow them down. I could throw rocks at it, but that wouldn't slow it down. If it did anything, it would hurt someone, and I didn't want to do that. I didn't think a stick could do much, plus there

SAMUEL PARIGELA

weren't a whole lot of random sticks lying around. I ran a couple inches behind the vehicle, and saw it start to move. I kicked the truck's side to try to make the driver stop, and I crouched down so the mirrors couldn't see me. Out of desperation, I felt for anything in my pockets that could help me, and my fingers landed on the multi-tool laser pointer. I quickly snapped out the knife part of the pointer and drove the blade through the back left tire. I twisted it around in there to make sure it penetrated.

I could hear the air rushing out, and as I stuffed the blade back into my pocket, a voice rang out:

"Hey! What do you think you're doing?" he said furiously. The man was wearing jeans, a white shirt, a blue blazer, and aviators. He seemed well-groomed, with a neatly shaven face and hair that was pulled back.

"I–Uh," I stopped and collected myself. This man stole the car, I didn't have to be afraid to approach him, I thought. So, I railed on him.

"What are *you* doing? Why are you stealing this truck?"

He laughed. "Stealing this truck? You think

I'm *stealing* this truck? You–" He paused, shaking his head smug. "Look, it's none of your business, kid. Why am I even talking to you?" He was about to get back in the truck when the Mayor appeared behind me. All of a sudden, the man looked afraid.

"Uh, Jerry!" He called, distressed. "This rat is trying to kill me! He got my car, look!" he said, gesturing to the hole in his tire.

"Willis? What are you... doing?" the mayor asked, his voice shaky and uncertain. This man was Willis?

"That's not the point, he damaged my car!" Willis said, trying to draw attention to what I did.

I sighed, frustrated. "That's not even your own car. That's carjacking!" I added. "We need those books, Willis."

"You need these books? Well, what about the bar? No one needs the bar? No one needs relaxation in their lives?" He was seething now. "Did you not see how many people went to the bar? It was so popular and successful. Why–and about that will, I could have kept it away in the ground fifty miles from here and you would have never found it."

"What matters is what the will says," I

remarked.

He grunted and shook his head, turning to the Mayor. "You were jealous, weren't you? You were jealous of my success. So you played dirty, huh?"

"What–no!" the Mayor was shocked.

"Yeah? Then why did you decide to be a politician instead of taking the library? 'Cause there's less money in the library. Less power."

"No, I just thought I couldn't handle two things at once," the mayor responded. "Then why did you convert the library to a bar? Because there's more money there, right?"

Willis huffed and got back into the truck as I yelled, "You're back at it again? How are you going to drive with a flat tire?"

He didn't respond, but hit the gas and started to take off. He was still going slow enough, however, that I could hop onto the truck bed if I ran fast enough. I ran towards the truck preparing my body to leap, and as soon as I was about to jump, my head hit an arm–the rough fabric of a suit jacket-covered arm. I fell to the ground upon impact. I grunted as I got up, and my body sank when I saw the truck–and its lopsided tire–speed down the road.

I looked up to see the mayor standing over me, but watching the truck disappear into the distance. I expected him to say 'sorry' or something, but I received no apology, so I was confused.

"Mr. Mayor?"

He stepped away from me as I started to get up.

"You can call me Mr. *Caddel*," he said, sharply. "Quit chasing this library fantasy of yours, Dan. No one gets any real entertainment out of a library."

"What?"

"You wouldn't understand!" he said, louder. "You're twelve years old, for crying out loud."

"Yeah, I don't understand. I don't understand what you're saying all of sudden."

"I'm saying the library is useless, are you slow?" He was softer now, a vicious harmlessness. "I'm a Caddel, too, Dan. I go by a different name to separate myself from them, but it is what it is."

I was shaking from fear and resentment. It was bitter. Bitter betrayal.

And I said it out loud: "You... betrayed me."

"Betrayed?" he asked, grinning sinisterly. "I was never on your side in the first place." He looked above me, to the library.

"You basically helped me raise money to build a casino. I'll do what I want with this place. and it'll be great. The books will make for vintage decorations. Watch me turn this library into the biggest social scene in town."

"No!" I cried out.

"I don't care! Listen to me; I. Used. You. I never cared, Dan, and no one will. You're just a kid."

I was silent. I had nothing to say. I walked back into the library, and found my parents. We walked home early, before the festivities ended.

CHAPTER 24: MY VILLAIN ORIGIN STORY
The Mayor

It wasn't personal, really. I simply had my own interests in mind–doesn't everybody? Who, in their right minds, would shut down a ludicrous business for *community bonding*? When I hired little Dan as an intern, I knew what I was doing. The kid had a knack for community service, and my savior complex found this to be the perfect little project to boost my ratings. Reelection would be a breeze with a little altruism–altered to cater to the alcoholics.

Sitting in the dimly lit study of my lavish mayoral residence, I allowed my thoughts to drift back to the events that led me to become the two-faced leader I had become. It was a reflection upon the twisted path that brought me here, where the pursuit of personal gain overshadowed any semblance of morality or genuine altruism.

Memories from my childhood resurfaced, revealing a pivotal event that had shaped my understanding of the power of manipulation. It was a warm summer day, and the annual Oakridge Fair was in full swing. Throngs of people filled the fairgrounds, their laughter and excitement creating an atmosphere of joy.

SAMUEL PARIGELA

Amidst the colorful booths and lively attractions, a crowd had gathered around a mesmerizing magic show. Interested, I squeezed my way through, eager to witness the spectacle. A charismatic magician named Jonathan took center stage, commanding the attention of young and old alike.

Jonathan possessed an uncanny ability to captivate the audience with his illusions, making objects disappear and reappear at will. But it wasn't just his magic tricks that fascinated me–it was the way he manipulated the crowd's emotions.

I watched as Jonathan skillfully manipulated their perception of reality, utilizing misdirection and subtle psychological cues. He elicited gasps of astonishment and applause, making them believe they were witnessing something extraordinary. It was a revelation, an awakening to the power of manipulation.

In that moment, I realized that people could be swayed, controlled even, through the art of deception. Jonathan, with his silver tongue and calculated charm, had effortlessly influenced the emotions and thoughts of the entire audience. I was captivated by the control he held over their perceptions and actions.

From that day forward, I became acutely aware of the potential power hidden within manipulation. I saw how it could be wielded as a tool to shape reality, to achieve personal gain, and to attain positions of authority. It was a revelation that simultaneously intrigued and disturbed me, igniting a spark within me–an insatiable desire to master the art of manipulation for my own benefit.

Over the years, I honed my skills, observing the tactics of influential figures in various spheres of life. I studied their methods, their nuances, and their ability to adapt to different situations. I learned that by wearing different masks and manipulating the perceptions of others, I could navigate the complex web of power and influence with ease.

And so, as I reminisced on that fateful day at the Oakridge Fair, I recognized the defining moment that had set me on the path of manipulation. Like I said, it wasn't personal; it was a realization that survival in this world required one to be cunning, adaptable, and willing to exploit the vulnerabilities of others.

But now, as the consequences of my actions loomed large, I couldn't help but wonder if the power I had obtained through manipulation was worth the price I had paid. The trust of the community had eroded, leaving me isolated and filled with regret. The echoes of that childhood revelation reverberated through the study, a haunting reminder of the darkness that lay within me. I had to do something to weasel my way out of this situation.

CHAPTER 25: AFTERMATH
Dan

I stopped going to the Mayor's office and took a break from going to the library after that incident. While I didn't go back to the office, I decided to go to the library after a week. After all, it was technically my creation, and despite what the Mayor had said, I was in no way going to stand by and watch it crumble. When I came back, I decided to visit the café on the way to see how it was doing. I walked up the stairs, but I couldn't yet smell the coffee at the usual halfway mark. Perhaps lower production? I reached the top of the flight of stairs and looked around for the café. I saw it, but what I found surprised me–a small 21+ sign in front of the café. Next to the sign was a public notice that said that the establishment had obtained approval from the city to sell... alcohol? What?

Afraid to see the Mayor again, I decided to stop by Mr. Strellis' room.

"The café, Mr. Strellis! What happened?" I exclaimed sitting in a chair across from him.

"We just transitioned it into being a bar, to better serve everyone, both the library-goers and bar advocates."

SAMUEL PARIGELA

"How do you expect to have a bar in a library, that just doesn't make sense!"

He shrugged. "It's really nothing new. The people here have enough sense to not interrupt the library. It will be fine, Dan."

"But the whole point was to get rid of the bar. And drunk people have no sense."

"It's the middle ground, Dan. You can't always have your own way, it just doesn't work like that." He saw my defeated posture and continued: "It only takes up a fourth of the second floor. It really won't be that bad."

There were more people at the new bar than at the check-out. In fact, there were so many people who came to the bar, that many library goers stopped coming to the library on account that the people at the bar were relatively noisy and seemed to take up the entire library despite only being in a small portion of it. Mr. Strellis ignored it, and acted like everything was fine. I didn't bother to go back to him; apparently the Mayor had convinced him too.

I thought of all the children who had been so excited to enjoy a library for the first time–myself included. Our dreams were wrecked by the money-grabbing, alcohol-motivated men in suits.

CHAPTER 26: TOO MUCH TRUST

Dan

The summer sun beat down upon the streets, its golden rays painting the town in a warm glow. I walked to Dingerman's, contemplating my next move in the battle against the Mayor's sinister plans, and maybe to buy some soaps–I was running low. Lost in my thoughts, I failed to notice the approach of Mr. Fitzpatrick, the enigmatic and gruff math teacher who had always maintained an air of mystery. I can't believe I missed him, Mr. Fitzpatrick dressed in a neon-green tracksuit.

"Dan," Mr. Fitzpatrick called out, his voice surprisingly gentle. Startled, I turned to face him, my eyes widening at the unexpected encounter. His scraggly facial hair framed a weathered face, giving him an aura of experience and wisdom.

"I've been watching your efforts to save the library," he continued, his words laced with a hint of sincerity. "You have a fire within you, a passion for something greater than yourself."

His unexpected praise caught me off guard. I had always regarded Mr. Fitzpatrick as an enigma, an eccentric figure who barely uttered more than a few words in class. Yet here he stood, acknowledging my determination to protect the heart of our town.

"I believe in your cause," he whispered, his eyes gleaming with a hidden intensity. "But there are forces at play that you cannot comprehend."

Confusion mingled with curiosity as Mr. Fitzpatrick extended an invitation. "Come with me, Dan," he urged, his voice a mere whisper in the bustling streets. "There is something you need to see."

With a mixture of trepidation and a sliver of trust, I followed Mr. Fitzpatrick to his car, the brightness of the day contrasting with the growing unease within me. The minutes stretched into eternity as the car rumbled along, the silence between us punctuated by the hum of the engine.

We arrived at the back of the library, where the entrance to the basement of the now-infamous bar had once stood. It was a place that held memories of laughter and community, now tainted by the specter of destruction. Mr. Fitzpatrick motioned for me to follow him, his footsteps echoing in the stillness.

My heart pounded within my chest as

he guided me deeper into the shadows, where the basement's dark secrets awaited. A sense of foreboding hung in the air as he halted abruptly, a large cabinet standing before us.

"Dan," Mr. Fitzpatrick said gruffly, his voice laced with a touch of regret. "The Mayor didn't like you tattling to Mr. Strellis, and wants you to keep your mouth shut. I hope you've learned your lesson." With a swift motion, he pushed me into the cabinet, its doors locking with a resounding click. The world around me dissolved into darkness, leaving me trapped and bewildered.

Through the muffled sounds outside the cabinet, I caught Mr. Fitzpatrick's grumble, his words barely reaching my ears. "The Mayor didn't pay me nearly enough for this," he muttered.

Locked away in the confining space, I was left with my thoughts. Really depressed thoughts.

CHAPTER 27: PICK A LOCK, SAVE A FRIEND
Lukas

As I observed Dan's encounter with Mr. Fitzpatrick near Dengel's Shop, a sense of unease washed over me. I knew there was something fishy about that teacher, and seeing Dan willingly climb into his car only heightened my suspicions. Instinctively, I decided to follow them, my curiosity piqued and a nagging feeling that Dan was in danger.

I trailed them from a safe distance, blending into the background as I watched their every move. My mind raced, analyzing the situation and devising a plan. I knew I had to act swiftly and use my smarts to get Dan out of this mess.

As Mr. Fitzpatrick parked the car near the back entrance of the library, I hid behind a nearby tree, silently observing their every move. My heart pounded in my chest as Mr. Fitzpatrick forcefully shoved Dan into the basement entrance of the bar, sealing his fate within a large cabinet. Anger boiled within me, fueled by the injustice of it all. Dan didn't deserve this.

I waited for Mr. Fitzpatrick, my once-beloved

fashion icon and now second-most-disliked human in town, to leave. He looked rather upset about what he had just done. As he should be, honestly.

Quickly and quietly, I slid into the basement, met with a large, jangling cabinet. Dan was struggling, pounding against the door.

"Dan, it's me, Lukas! Stay still, okay?" I hoped Dan would calm down a little. Lock-picking requires the utmost concentration.

The cabinet stopped shaking.

Drawing upon my extensive knowledge of locks and my arsenal of contraptions, I approached the cabinet with determination. The familiar sound of gears falling into place reverberated in the dimly lit basement as I deftly picked the lock. The door swung open, revealing a stunned and grateful Dan.

"How did you do that?" Dan asked, his eyes wide with amazement.

I shrugged nonchalantly, trying to hide my pride. "Oh, you know, just a little something I picked up along the way. No big deal."

I led Dan out of the basement and we walked

into the "library", his eyes taking in the sight of the bar with a mix of sadness and disappointment. Sensing his despondency, I placed a comforting hand on his shoulder.

"Dan, sometimes it feels like us kids don't have a say in the world. People dismiss us, thinking we don't understand or that our ideas don't matter. But don't let that stop you from fighting for what you believe in," I advised, my voice tinged with a hint of wisdom beyond my years.

We made our way back to his home, navigating the streets with caution. As we approached his front door, I paused, turning to face him. The weight of the world seemed to rest upon his young shoulders, and I couldn't help but admire his determination.

"Dan, keep living your life. Keep hoping, even when it feels like the bad guys always win. Trust me, the good guys take over in the end," I assured him, my voice filled with conviction.

His eyes met mine, gratitude and admiration shining through. "Thanks, Lukas. I couldn't have done any of this without you."

I smiled, genuine and warm. "You've done a real incredible job, Dan. Remember, no matter how much I've acted all great and popular at school, you're the real role model here."

Before he entered the house, I offered a final piece of advice. "Dan, it might be better not to tell your parents about what happened. The mayor is... kind of crazy, and who knows what he could do if the news gets out. Besides, you were only locked in for a few minutes."

Dan nodded.

"You know, Dan, getting into strange people's cars isn't usually my thing. I'm a lot smarter than that," I quipped, a mischievous glint in my eye.

Dan chuckled, his laughter mingling with a sense of gratitude. "Yeah, I guess I still have a lot to learn from you, Lukas."

With a final nod, I turned to leave, waiting a moment as Dan stepped inside his home.

CHAPTER 28: LEGAL TROUBLE 2.0
Mr. Fitzpatrick

The air was heavy with the weight of my actions as I stood in the dimly lit room, my heart pounding with a mixture of guilt and regret. Dan, a mere pawn in this sinister game, was stuck inside the cabinet. The echo of his muffled cries still reverberated in my ears, a haunting reminder of the path I had chosen.

Loneliness had always been my faithful companion, but in that moment, it felt suffocating, a suffocating reminder of my own emptiness. The euphoria I had hoped to find in the execution of this heinous act had been replaced by a gnawing sense of self-disgust. I had allowed myself to be consumed by the allure of money, my bitterness blinding me to the consequences of my actions.

As the reality of what I had done sank in, a pang of remorse tore through my bitter facade. This was not the man I aspired to be. This was not the legacy I had intended to leave behind. But it was too late for regrets. The deed was done, and now, the consequences would follow.

In a haze of desperation, I made my way to

the mayor's office. The man behind the image of power and influence would be the one to answer for this travesty. With each step, my bitterness morphed into a toxic cocktail of anger and disappointment.

Pushing open the heavy wooden door, I found Mr. Mayor seated behind his imposing desk, his demeanor oozing with false charm. His gaze met mine, a glint of complacent satisfaction flickering in his eyes.

"What brings you here, Mr. Fitzpatrick?" he inquired, his voice dripping with calculated civility.

"This is all wrong!" I seethed. "What have you gotten me into?"

Mr. Mayor leaned back in his chair, a smug smile stretching across his face. "Keep your mouth shut, Fitzpatrick," he sneered. "You've been paid handsomely for your services. Not just with this kid, but plenty more. Don't let your conscience get in the way now."

His words stung, fueling the anger that had been simmering within me. But I knew deep down that I couldn't continue down this treacherous path. The bitterness had consumed me for far too long, and it was time to confront the consequences of my choices.

Leaving the mayor's office, I made my way to the local police station. The weight of guilt bore down on my shoulders as I entered the building, a strange mix of determination and resignation guiding my steps. I approached the nearest officer, my voice trembling with a mixture of fear and regret.

"I've done something terrible," I confessed, my bitterness seeping into each word. "I've kidnapped a young man and been paid by corrupt officials to do much more. I need to turn myself in."

The officers led me to an interrogation room, their eyes filled with a mixture of suspicion and curiosity. As they processed my surrender, a glimmer of confusion crossed their faces.

"Wait a minute," one of the officers said, scrutinizing my appearance. "Aren't you the guy we arrested some time ago? The one who looked a lot like this math teacher?"

I was confused. Huh? The police officers tugged at my mustache and hair, trying to see if they would come off. They must have been crazy.

Ignoring the strange behavior of the

officers, I showed them the incriminating email correspondence between myself and the mayor. The trail of evidence painted a vivid picture of the mayor's involvement in this nefarious plot.

Their expressions changed from suspicion to realization as they read through the emails, their eyes widening with each passing sentence. The truth was unraveling before them–the mayor felt threatened by Dan and his ability to create change, and wanted to scare him so he'd stay out of the way.

Determined to save Dan, we ventured out into the night, our footsteps echoing through the empty streets. But as we arrived at the location where Dan was supposed to be, we were met with an empty room, a lingering trace of his presence. He had escaped!

A sense of bitter satisfaction welled up within me as the officers acknowledged my innocence. While I was glad for Dan, I couldn't help but think that I had one job and couldn't even make sure the lock would stay on.

Dan had eluded capture, but the revelation of the mayor's involvement sparked a new fire within them. They would pursue justice, investigating the very man who had orchestrated this tangled web of deceit.

As they prepared to dig deeper into the mayor's affairs, I was allowed to walk away, a free man burdened by the knowledge of my own shortcomings. In that moment, I felt a sense of twisted pride. I had taken responsibility for my actions, and the truth was finally coming to light.

I had done the right thing, even if it was born out of bitterness and self-loathing. And now, justice would have its day, even as the darkness threatened to consume us all.

CHAPTER 29: PEOPLE CHANGE

Dan

After talking to Lukas, I walked in to see my Grandfather in the living room.

"Grandpa!"

"Oh, Dan! Well, hello there," he said, hugging me.

"I have some bad news for you." I frowned.

He looked concerned. "What?"

"There's a new bar in the library now. It's what I've worked so hard to get rid of."

Grandpa looked at me over his glasses. "Dan, come on now. There's gotta be some sort of middle ground, some sort of compromise in every situation."

I was shocked. "But, Grandpa, you were the one–"

"I know, I was the one who said the bar is bad and we have to get rid of it, yes. But like I said–

middle ground. One can't always have their way."

I let go of his arm, discouraged.

"I'll see you later, young man." he said, giving me a fist-bump and standing up.

"Well, where are you going?" I asked, tired.

"I want to see what's so great about the bar over at the library..."

"Grandpa! What?"

"I'm just going to check it out, Dan, I'll see you."

I watched in shock as my grandfather walked out the way I came in, because he wanted to "check out" not books, but some drinks.

"What. What," This was. Absolute insanity.

CHAPTER 30: TIME DOESN'T HEAL ALL WOUNDS
Dan

As the years passed, the wounds of betrayal and disillusionment remained etched deep within my soul. Months of toil and unwavering dedication had birthed a vision I believed would revolutionize minds and hearts. But the bitter reality I faced was far from the dream I once held close.

The library, my cherished creation, stood neglected, a mere shadow of its potential. Its halls echoed with the whispers of forgotten wisdom, drowned out by the clamor of a bustling bar nearby and the opulent allure of casinos and clubs that sprouted like weeds in the surrounding area. The city had succumbed to the allure of quick monetary gain, discarding intellectual nourishment and genuine growth like discarded scraps.

In moments of introspection, I still questioned myself relentlessly. Could I have done more to safeguard the sanctity of knowledge? Would additional flyers or a broader network have shielded my creation from the rapid descent into corruption? I was just a child, but the weight of responsibility pressed upon my fragile shoulders, burdened by the realization that the world could be a heartless and cruel place.

With every book read, every idea shared, I vowed to restore the library to its rightful place–a beacon of knowledge, a sanctuary for the seekers of truth. For in the face of heartlessness, the unwavering pursuit of compassion and enlightenment becomes an act of defiance. And as I carried the torch of hope through the darkened corridors of the forgotten, I realized that within this struggle lay the essence of my own growth, my own resilience, and my own redemption.

CHAPTER 31: A SECOND CHANCE
Dan

The summer sun cast a warm glow over the small town as I looked out the window sitting on the living room sofa, feeling the weight of another completed school year finally lifting from my shoulders. Sophomore year had been challenging, but it was nothing compared to the battles I had fought within myself over the state of our beloved library.

Ever since that fateful day when the mayor and his corrupt government had turned our once amazing sanctuary of knowledge into a den of vice, I had felt a fire burning deep within me. The library had always been my refuge, my escape from the mundane world. To see it reduced to a center for alcoholics and gamblers felt like a personal betrayal. Even my own grandfather, who had guided my and taken such an interest in my efforts couldn't resist the temptations offered by the bars, casinos, and clubs that had been planted throughout the town.

Lost in my thoughts, I was startled by a knock on the door. Opening it, I found myself face to face with my best friend, Lukas Tinderdale.

Lukas had been by my side through it all, sharing my frustrations and dreams of reclaiming the library for the community. But today, he had brought reinforcements.

Behind Lukas stood a group of familiar faces, all wearing expressions of resolute determination. There was Leah, a quiet and thoughtful girl who always had a way of seeing things from a different perspective. Adam, with his infectious energy and knack for making people laugh. And Kian, a shy but brilliant young mind who had a thirst for knowledge.

"Dan, we've been talking," Lukas began, his voice filled with a renewed sense of purpose. "We can't let the city's corruption keep us down. We've been thinking about the library, and we want to try again to topple the corrupt hold that the city has on it. We believe that a large group of people would be more powerful than a boy all by himself."

I stood there, captivated by the unwavering determination in their eyes. It was as if they had breathed life into my very thoughts. I had spent countless nights envisioning a brighter future for the library, and now, here stood a group of like-minded people ready to join me in this endeavor.

"What can we do?" I asked, my voice filled

with a mix of excitement and trepidation.

Lukas smiled, his eyes gleaming with confidence. "First, we need to gather support from the community. We need to show them that the library can be so much more than what it has become. We can reach out to the churches and after-school programs, organize events, and spread the word."

As we sat down on my porch, our conversation filled with ideas and plans, my mind couldn't help but wander to the memories I had of the library before it fell into disarray. I remembered visiting with my grandfather, eagerly listening to his stories and marveling at the vast collection of books. However, before I could pursue the library, there was something I needed to do.

Dingerman's was a familiar place. It had become a regular stop for me after school to pick up snacks or school supplies. As I entered the store, the smell of the newest shipment of soap and the sound of the door chime filled the air. I made my way to the counter, where Mr. Dingerman, the store owner, greeted me with a warm smile.

"Hey, Dan! What can I get for you today?" he asked, his eyes crinkling with genuine kindness.

"Hey, Mr. Dingerman. Just a few things for now," I replied, scanning the shelves for some notebooks and pens, and seeing only soap. "Oh, and do you happen to know where my grandfather is? I wanted to talk to him."

Mr. Dingerman's smile faded slightly, and a touch of concern crossed his face. "Your grandfather? He's been spending a lot of time at the bar lately. You might find him there... I hope everything's okay."

My heart sank at his words. I had hoped that my grandfather would be at Dingerman's, but it seemed that he still couldn't get out of his habits. I thanked Mr. Dingerman for the information and purchased the items I needed including 6 soaps of every variety, all the while carrying a heavy weight of disappointment.

With a determined sigh, I headed toward the bar, which had initially been housed in the area of the library that had been the café but had grown in size (and popularity) to dominate much of the building. The sign outside read "The Old Pages," a cruel reminder of what had been lost. Since the establishment was *technically* a library, there was no ID requirement to enter–just to purchase drinks. However, this place was usually filled with adults, not a single child to be found with a picture book in his or her lap. I pushed open the heavy wooden door, bracing myself for the sight that awaited me.

The bar was dimly lit, the air thick with the scent of alcohol and the murmur of conversations. Hundreds of books lined the walls, but no one read them–they were simply for decoration at this point. As expected, no kids. I spotted my grandfather sitting alone at the far end of the bar, lost in his own thoughts. With hesitant steps, I approached him, the clinking of glasses and laughter filling the background.

"Grandpa," I said, my voice barely audible above the noise.

He turned to look at me, his eyes bloodshot and weary. "Dan? What are you doing here?"

"I... I wanted to talk to you," I stammered, struggling to find the right words. "The library, it's fallen into ruin again . We're trying to change that, to bring it back to life. Will you join us?"

For a moment, there was silence, as if the weight of my words hung in the air. My grandfather's gaze softened, a flicker of recognition crossing his eyes. "Dan, I'm sorry," he said, his voice filled with regret. "I've let you down, and I've let myself down. Maybe I can make things right soon. I don't know, but I'll try."

The realization that my grandfather still held a glimmer of hope brought a surge of warmth to my heart. Perhaps this journey to reclaim the library would not only be about the physical space but also about the healing and redemption of those who had lost their way.

I left the bar, the conversations and clinking glasses fading into the background. I felt a renewed sense of purpose as I rejoined Lukas and the others, ready to continue our mission. We spent the day brainstorming and planning, knowing that our journey to rebuild the library was not just about bricks and mortar but about rebuilding a community's spirit.

In the days that followed, more boys and girls joined our cause. We held community meetings, organized book drives and fundraisers, and even staged small plays to raise awareness. Every step we took brought us closer to our goal of toppling the corrupt hold on the library and restoring it to its rightful place as a center of knowledge and community.

As I look back on that day, years later, I can't help but feel a sense of pride and fulfillment. It wasn't easy, and it still isn't–we continue to face the same opposition we did years ago. But now we have the community behind us. The library may not have been physically rebuilt during that time, but something far more powerful was constructed–the bond of a community united by a shared vision. It was something of a moral revival, and it continues today.

In that moment, surrounded by friends who had become family, I felt an indomitable spirit rising within me. We were determined, excited, and filled with hope. Together, we were unstoppable.

And as the sun began to set on that summer evening, I stood on the porch, the cool breeze carrying the whispers of possibility. The day's discussions and plans had ignited a fire within me, propelling me forward. The journey to reclaim the library was just beginning, but I knew, deep within my heart, that we would succeed. It wouldn't be a simple path–the library would fall into the hands of the wrong people every now and then, but with every failure, the following successes were stronger.

I felt a surge of determination and excitement coursing through my veins. With the support of my newfound friends, unwavering belief of my parents, and the conviction of our community, I was ready to face the challenges ahead. Together, we would write a new chapter for our town, one filled with hope, knowledge, and the triumph of the human spirit–one brick at a time.

EPILOGUE

As I reflect upon the story of Dan's journey to rebuild the library, I am reminded of the stories of some real-life heroes from which I drew inspiration. While the outcome of the story might not align with the narrative of triumph, it is precisely in the face of challenges and apparent failures that we find valuable lessons to shape our own lives.

In the spirit of transparency and authenticity, I must acknowledge that Dan's story did not conclude with the resounding success I initially envisioned. Just as many of my real-life heroes faced setbacks and obstacles along their path, Dan also encountered his fair share of trials and tribulations.

Dan was a visionary with a deep-rooted belief in the transformative power of knowledge and the importance of community. He embarked on a mission to rebuild our neglected library, igniting hope and enthusiasm among the townspeople. His dedication and unwavering commitment were evident as he poured his heart and soul into the restoration project.

Despite the setbacks and the ultimate

realization that the library's restoration might not come to fruition in the way we had hoped, Dan's journey is not one of failure but of resilience and personal growth. It is through his struggles that we find redemption and valuable lessons to carry forward.

Dan's unwavering determination in the face of mounting challenges is a testament to the strength of the human spirit. He refused to succumb to despair, focusing instead on the positive impact his efforts had already made within the community.

In our journey to rebuild the library, we encountered moments of unexpected grace and support; strangers rallied to our cause, offering their time, skills, and resources. Volunteers poured in, passionate about restoring the library's legacy. These moments of connection and generosity highlighted the transformative power of community and the indomitable spirit of unity.

While the physical restoration of the library may not have been fully realized, the journey itself became a catalyst for personal growth, collective inspiration, and a deeper understanding of the power of hope and resilience. Through our shared experiences, we discovered the importance of cherishing what we have, embracing the rebuilding process, and finding solace in the bonds we forge along the way.

Ultimately, the true measure of success lies not in attaining a specific outcome but in the lessons we glean from our trials and our impact on those around us. Dan's story serves as a poignant reminder that our journeys are not defined solely by external accomplishments but by the transformation that takes place within ourselves and our community.

Dear reader, I invite you to reflect upon Dan's story and find solace in the lessons it imparts. May it inspire you to persevere in the face of adversity, embrace the journey rather than fixate on the destination, and recognize that true growth and redemption often arise from unexpected places.

Instead of looking back, therefore, we shall look forward.

With gratitude and a renewed sense of purpose,

Samuel P.